HUSTLING AGAINST THE ODDS

A Tell-All about the Truth of the American Dream

An Autobiography

Jarrel L. Johnson

First Edition

PAGE PUBLISHING, INC.
New York, NY

First originally published by Page Publishing, Inc. 2017

ISBN 978-1-63568-594-7 (Paperback)
ISBN 978-1-63568-595-4 (Digital)

Printed in the United States of America

FOREWORD

Through my journey in life thus far, I have accomplished a lot, and there have been those who have played in a role in that. I would like to thank my immediate family and my daughter, Leeona Johnson, who provides me with the motivation to keep thriving today. I would like to thank my mother, Angela Townsend Johnson, in particular, for providing me with support and belief in my abilities throughout my life. I would like to thank my father, Dr. Ronnie Lee Johnson, who installed in me a relentless will and priceless knowledge that I have been able to apply to life thus far. I also wrote this in memory of my Grandmother Dorothy "Cookie" Townsend, who was another believer in my talents and recently passed away from cancer. I would also like to acknowledge two grandfathers who have passed away Robert Lee "Muffin" Johnson, the seed from which I came, and Willie "Big Bo" C. Townsend, both of which were great men who stood in a world that would have them sit down. I would like to thank the friends I have met along my journey thus far that have provided me with an opportunity, whether that has been a job, a position, or a gift; and finally, any other family and friends that have been true supporters of my journey.

CONTENTS

CHAPTER 1

Introduction: What Is Hustling Against the Odds?

No opportunity around me, no hope—only the factories awaited me, no growth—only a recycled process for me, no wealth—only minimum wage awaited me, only a town—no big city around me, no real hustlers—only haters around me, no trust fund—only paycheck-to-paycheck awaited me, no advancements—only glass ceilings awaited me; this was the path that awaited me. But as I write this, I have stayed in ten different cities and five different states. I have visited another country. I am a high school graduate. I started as a varsity basketball player—my senior year averaging around ten points and ten rebounds a game—played college basketball, played college football, earned an academic scholarship to go to college, earned a university athletic scholarship, and ranked fifteen in the nation for forced fumbles concluding my senior collegiate year at Central Washington University according to NCAA rankings. I attended a pro day at the university in which I earned my athletic scholarship, attended the 2013 NFL Regional Combine at the Seattle Seahawks Training Facility in which I was selected following my workout to do an interview with Q13 Fox News, was recruited by the Columbus Lions of the Professional Indoor Football League to continue my career as a professional football player, and performed as an athlete in arenas around the world. I am a college graduate with two AA degrees, one of which is in arts and humanities and the other in elementary education teacher preparation. I have a daughter who is one year of age, going on two. I broke through some barriers; none of these things were meant for me to accomplish, coming from where I came from. I couldn't have accomplished a portion of these things without some persistent hustle, hustling against odds stacked solid against me, being a black man who didn't come from much in America.

What exactly does it mean to hustle well? Most dictionaries will tell you something of this nature: *Hustle*—a verb meaning to urge or move hurriedly along; to work busily and quickly; (slang) to make energetic efforts to solicit business or make money. What are *odds*? Well, most dictionaries will tell you something of this nature: *Odds*—a noun meaning a ratio between the probability against and the probability for something happening or being true. So what did "hustling against the odds" mean for me? Here is my definition of "hustling against the odds" from a real-life point of view based on my actual life events.

CHAPTER 2

No Opportunity Coming from Where I Came from

Growing up in a small town, I can remember even as a child that chances were slim and opportunities where few. Bennettsville, South Carolina, raised me. Coming from Bennettsville, a city with a current population of around 9,400 (2014), it's not common that you make it out. There, jobs are limited, and the inner city is poor, and the overall city has little infrastructure compared to most modern-day cities (we just got a Wal-Mart in the year 2013). I never knew that one day I would have college degrees, be a scholarship athlete, be able to leave the country, show the world my talents, and stand before cameras.

I was raised by a father who had great leadership qualities. He was a hustler, and he had great business skills—just an overall brilliant conscious mind. So much he had to give to the world, so much to offer, for growth, for building, for development, a lot of which came from his own life experiences. But he still was a poor man, financially, according to America's typical average income per household. He too had been raised by a man who came from very little and made a way to provide for a family of eight with little to pass on to the next generation. Mainly just knowledge he had acquired from his own life experiences, and that is what my father passed to me as well. My father had dreams of playing professional basketball but had his first son, my older brother, shortly after high school. So college wasn't an option (that, and my mother saying that she needed him there with her). My father wanted us, his family, not to want for anything, to live comfortably. So he worked extremely hard in different manufacturing plants here and there; my mother did the same right along his side. They still found themselves living from paycheck to paycheck, struggling to make ends meet with no promising future ahead. Then I came along, and soon behind me were my younger sister and younger brother. Something had to give. How do you build, financially, with no proven education to back a good job? How do you grow and achieve your goals in life when you don't have the time, finances, or knowhow to do so? How do you build and plan a future for your kids so that they too can grow and leave priceless knowledge to their children as well as leave tangible assets that they've acquired from a productive life? Leave these things for their children and for their children to leave to their children and their children to their children and for generations to come to build upon, for continuous progress in a world that demands it. How do you not get left behind? How do you do these things when all your time goes to survival, surviving for yourself and your family?

My father thought about these things often. So most times, when he opened his mouth to talk to us, it was to tell us valuable information. He was giving us—me, my brothers, and my sister—knowledge and wisdom, knowledge and wisdom we needed to get through life. My father taught my brothers and me how to play the board game chess growing up. He was pretty good at it. He would take his queen, the most powerful piece on the board as far as move-making and being a threat was concerned, off the board and still beat us. There were a lot of lessons in him taking his queen off the board, a lot of knowledge and wisdom that we could later use in life. My father had decided to pursue a better life for us and his family, a decision that ended up in a two-year-and-some-months prison sentence and a felony record for life. This was an option he had chosen, given the circumstances he was dealt, playing this game called life with the cards he had been dealt. I was in the second or third grade when they came and locked my father up for selling drugs when they came and boarded up the windows on our house, when they came and took all our furniture and clothes, all our toys, and Christmas gifts our father had brought for us. I remember when my mom would take me, my brother and my sister and drive by our house we once lived in (while my father was in prison), and it was still boarded up, and by this time, the grass had grown up around the house as tall the house itself, and my mom would say, "One day, y'all, we will move back in." I believed her, but the idea seemed so farfetched, seeing what was before me.

As a boy growing up, my father geared me toward basketball, seeing that I was very athletic and he too was good at the game. He and my mother pushed for my grades to be great because they saw that I too had a brilliant mind. My mom tells a story that when I was a very young child before I even started going to school that I came to her and told her I could add up numbers in my head. She didn't believe me, so I started calling out numbers and adding them up in my head; she was amazed. But I did exactly what they wanted me to. I placed in high-level classes throughout grade school. Early in school, I often achieved highest average awards in different subjects, all As and A and B honor roll achievements. As I got older, I made the junior high basketball team and basketball became a game I wanted to conquer. I wanted to study the best and be even better with the natural athletic abilities God gave me. I had many other talents besides being a good academic and good at basketball. I was a very talented artist; my ability to draw very well was noticeable at an early age. I was athletic enough to play any sport, not only basketball. But there was no room for growing my other talents. Besides the fact that I never grew up seeing any African Americans (black people), being an artist and making enough money to move their family out the inner city, nor did any of my family draw for a living. I just saw working people keeping their head down to get by. My father geared me toward basketball and not any other sport because it was a game that he was familiar with; he could show me the things he had learned.

As I continued to get older, I began to realize that what was easier, more than anything, was to get my hands on drugs and guns, to pursue my wants and needs. This baffled me because these were the same things that everyone was telling me to avoid and that would be detrimental to my life. But how were these things so easily accessible to me? As I got older, my city grew in violence and drug activity by the year. But my father knew all too well about the statistics that lay before me as an African American in America. So while we were growing up, he also showed my brothers and me how to invest money and make a profit legally. He showed us how to invest money and start our own business. He showed us that an African American could own and operate his own business despite what we saw around us. He owned and operated two clothing stores of his own after prison. It's actually a funny story how he got into the clothing business. When he got locked up, it was hard for him to provide for us like he once did or even at all. So my father came up with the idea to sell the clothes he still had that he had acquired from hustling in the streets. My brother had hit an early growth spurt and could wear some of my father's clothes. So when we came to visit my dad in prison during visitation, my brother would have on multiple outfits, my father's clothes underneath. My brother would go into the restroom and take my father's clothes off and leave them in the stall. My father would make prior arrangements to sell them to other visitors and give the money to my mother before we left our visit. He was doing what he had to do. He picked up the trade, and to this day, he still sells clothes. After prison when he got himself back established in the world, he would take my brother and me along on road trips to Manhattan, New York. Manhattan was a great place to buy wholesale clothing. We had never seen anything like it; the city was booming with business and teeming with money. While we were still kids (my brother and me), he showed us how to network and conduct business with other businessmen. So my brother and I went from working under my father, selling clothes for him to investing in our own shipments/orders and turning over our own money for a profit. He was showing us this to keep us out of the streets so we didn't have to go down the dark road he did. I remember when I was about fourteen years old and I and my brother packed up our backpack with T-shirts my dad was selling, and we went out on foot, walking from door to door trying to sell our T-shirts. I and my brother made one hundred dollars that day, and it felt like we had made a million. One hundred dollars seemed like a lot for a country boy like me that had never seen much. And I kept all the money on me, all day. I myself by this time was filled with the "Go get it" attitude.

I always said to myself, "One day, I will make enough money to move my family out of this city and buy my parents a big nice house and they won't have to work anymore." I had seen them work so hard, and I felt like it would be well deserved. I saw that would be possible only by two ways. If I wanted to make enough money to do all of that, I had to make it as a professional basketball player or get big in the hustle game—this was clear even as a child that this was the reality I faced. Both were risks. Selling drugs, often referred to as hustling, was going to either put me in prison for a long time or I would end up losing my life. Working a regular 9–5 wasn't going to do it and getting a degree held no promises either. Even if I managed to put myself through school because my parents didn't have the money to do so, there was no guarantee that I would come out of college and get a high-salary-paying position. And from looking at the majority of people who held those positions, I clearly didn't fit the description. Or even being an entrepreneur like my dad, although he was able to run his own business, we still stayed in the inner city. The obvious choice, if I wanted to accomplish getting this big house for my mom and dad and retire them and build a future for myself so I could set a platform for my kids to build off, was I would have to make it as a professional athlete with my natural athletic ability. But even this was a risk, and I would have to risk everything I had just for the opportunity to become a professional athlete. I would be investing all the money I had, all the assets I had, all my time, and huge amounts of effort and energy. But I remembered how important my father and mother told me it was to "Get that education, son," so I never gave up on school. I continued to believe that that too was a way out. But I was no fool. I was very observant of my surroundings and the things that were going on in society concerning my family and other African American/black families.

I was in the fourth grade when I experienced my first act of blatant racism that I could remember. That racism came from my teacher Mrs. Midgley, a Caucasian/white lady. As I mentioned before, I was often placed in high-level classes, and I was placed in a high-level class during my fourth-grade year. From the beginning of the school year, it was clear that my teacher had something against me. I wasn't sure at the time what the predisposition was, whether it was because I was black or that my father was in prison at the time or what is was. It was evident from the way that she treated me and called my name during roll call in the mornings. I wasn't sure why; I was an innocent child for crying out loud. I thought maybe it was something I was doing wrong. My other twenty-something classmates were Caucasian, and many of them didn't take to me. I and a black girl were the only two black kids in the class, so we clung to each other naturally because of the circumstances. Mrs. Midgley would love to try to make me seem dumb in front of my other classmates, so I didn't raise my hand often. She never explained my homework or class work to me in depth; everything was brief and to the point, whether I understood it or not. She would try to make me feel out of place in several ways, day in and day out. I struggled that year academically, and it wasn't because I wasn't meant to be in those classes; it was simply because my "teacher" didn't feel I belonged there.

I remember one day while I was in the fourth grade, I had come home from school that day and I was playing out in the backyard. I found an old, dull, rusty kitchen knife buried in the ground as I was outside playing. It was like a treasure to me, so I put the knife in my coat pocket. I went to school that next day, and I had forgotten that I put the knife in my coat pocket. So during the day at school while in class, I put my coat up on my chair and the knife fell out. My teacher saw it; this was her time to shine. She moved all the kids to other side of the classroom and called in the principal. She picked up the knife with a napkin and put it in a plastic zip-lock bag. Here I was, nine or ten years old, and she was handling the "scene" like I just had committed murder or possibly could have. My father was locked up at this time, so my mom, grandmother, and my aunts all came up to the school because they were considering expelling me for the remainder of the school year and I would have to repeat the fourth grade. Even then I could not figure out what all the fuss was about. Here you have a bright student with no prior record of bad behavior in school and you want to expel him! You could not possibly have my best interest at heart. It angers me as I write this to relive that moment. But my relatives convinced the principal to give me a lighter "sentence," and I was suspended for a few days. What damage does that do to a child? The way my teacher treated me— what effect does that have on a child's confidence? How does that affect his or her decision making? Personally, in general, I think we take some of the smallest situations with our youth for granted. We should be careful how we speak and act around them because I feel the impact is deep and severe. I would find out later in life that the world was filled with Mrs. Midgleys. Everywhere I went, I was treated as if I was out of place or didn't belong as a minority, a black person, in America. I could go somewhere as simple as the convenient store and have a Caucasian (white person) serving me at the register and see things like them not wanting to touch my hand as I made my purchase. I would notice them drop my change in my hand to avoid contact. Things like this were common even as I left my city and stayed in other cities, even as I left my state and stayed in other states. When it seems as if the world doesn't accept you for what and who you really are, it makes you comfortable with being in the inner city and not want to venture out into the world and take risks to achieve true success. You would have to truly experience this to understand what I mean. When I say experience, I mean being a black person first of all. I could stay next door to a white person in the inner city and they would still not have experienced the life I had being in black skin. These were huge obstacles I faced as I went against the odds and ventured out into the world.

CHAPTER 3

The Pursuit of Opportunity

I continued to excel in basketball throughout grade school and continuously achieve high grades, but the streets were never too far, and that life continued to be easily accessible to me. Eventually I begin to engage in illegal activity to help me get through and get the things I needed and wanted in life. Just like I became very skilled in school, very skilled on the basketball court, and very skilled in business, I became a very skilled drug dealer. My father had never condoned any illegal activity from us and discouraged us from doing the things he had done, but it was almost like it was inevitable. And I was good at it, everything, I was good at the numbers, putting together good deals, and still making a profit. I was good at building up my clientele and keeping people coming back. I had a solid and consistent "connect" when I first started out, and I was good at keeping my connect paid. I was good at saving my money and not spending my "re-up" money, I was good at doubling up to bigger purchases, "getting my weight up." My neighborhood and surrounding neighborhoods had "crack-heads," "weed-heads," "cokeheads," you name it. So there was money to be made. I hit the block every day, and if my "homeboys" didn't have any work, that was even better because I keep work. I had a solid connect, and he had been in the game for quite some time, he kept work, and if he was out, then it wasn't long before he was "re-ing up" in a matter of hours. I was on, and it was hard to compete with me. I and others from the neighborhood and in the neighborhood had all kinds of hustles going. When we weren't "hitting a lick," we were gambling. I started to look forward to hustling the next day; the money was good and it was producing immediate results. How much money could I make this day? I had my clientele up so good that I would was waking up to forty to fifty dollars every day to start the day. Every $100 I made I would put in a rubber band and throw in my stash. I was able to buy cars and fix them up. I was able to give my mom money from time to time. I was able to go out of town to shop and eat wherever I wanted to. Life was all right, but the walls were closing in. I started noticing the police notice me. I notice that they knew what car I would be in and would tail me; I had a spot out in the country part of town where I could park my cars, so I started switching up cars. But even then, I could tell they were still able to monitor my activity. I starting hitting the block during the day on foot and riding my bike around town at night to make any "rounds" I had to make. I managed to stay under the radar, but still I knew that it wasn't going to last for long. So I was saving money and making plans to keep the ultimate goal alive. I started to notice my homeboys' jealousy toward me; as I got bigger, they either grew increasingly distant to me or stayed close and watched me with a jealous eye. When I came around, I wasn't so welcomed in the hood, but I came around anyway. It was where I was from, and no one was going to run me out of the neighborhood I grew up in. I started linking up with other hustlers from other neighborhoods, and we were networking and seeing where money could be made. I was taking a big risk at the time; I remember going to pick some work up from Highpoint, North Carolina, the next state over. This was a new connect I had met; I didn't really know whether he was going to be "solid" with me or not. I had three thousand dollars on me. He could have robbed me or killed me. I was meeting him on his turf in a spot that was far off any main streets and off in the "cut." I had one of my friends with me sitting in the car while I handled the deal and he was by my gun. But these were the kind of risk you had to take to stay competitive and keep the edge. It came with the game and was something I noticed even when I first got into that game. I saw so many pasts before me; friends that were my age that were getting shot and killed in this same game I was playing. Friends that were getting felony charges and getting locked up. I knew I had to stack money and get out. I got a job as a delivery driver at the local Pizza Hut to get some of the heat off me. I had got my weight up, but I was still catching every lick I could make. I had half pounds of weed, quarter pounds of weed, and grams of weed and hard bagged up in the car. Customers would call my cell phone for work, and when I would go out to deliver a pizza, I would meet with them really quick and go back to Pizza Hut. With that Pizza Hut delivery sign lit up on the top of my car, the police didn't even give me a second look. I ran that hustle until it was time for me to take the money I saved and make my next move. Selling drugs was/is nothing that I'm proud of, but coming from where I come from in life, what other good options do you have to make ways? There were kids my age living in the suburbs that couldn't imagine taking the risk I've taken and never had too, but instead they have already traveled the world and had the opportunity to open their mind to new worlds, network with others like them, have their way paid through college, get into the best of schools and venture into different businesses. Money that I was scraping up and risking my life and freedom for they could spend on one summer trip. Was it that their parents were harder working parents than mine? Was it because they had some type of entitlement that I or my parents didn't have in life?

Basketball, school, nor being an entrepreneur was producing any worthwhile immediate results, and hustling seemed to be the most productive thing I could do at the time to keep everything else afloat as far as putting myself through college to continue to play sports and educate myself. Hustling was a way to keep the dream/the goal alive. So even as I went off to college, I continued to hustle. I sold to other college students and even people that I met in the surrounding community. But to take a few steps back, as I mentioned before, I played basketball in junior high and was a starter. My talents were recognized by the coaches, my teammates, and people in the community. So as I entered into high school, I was already known to play basketball. My junior year, I went out for the varsity basketball team and I was cut and placed on the junior varsity team. My heart was crushed because I knew that if I had any chance of getting a descent college scholarship offer or any athletic college scholarship offer, I had to start building a repetition for myself at least by my junior year. I played junior varsity my junior year. But that following summer, my dad took me down to Myrtle Beach to play in some open gym runs; he had a friend that stayed in Myrtle Beach, South Carolina, and he and his sons were into sports as well. That friend knew the head basketball coach at Myrtle Beach High School and invited me to come and play in some open gym runs where other Myrtle Beach High School varsity players would be; the coach would be there as well. So my dad took me there to play, and the coach was very impressed with what he saw that day. I had a very productive day, and I shined amongst the other players there. By this time in my life, my athletic ability had flourished. I could jump from right inside of the free throw line and dunk a basketball with ease. I jump with great coordination off one or two feet. I played well above the rim. If you missed a shot on my team, I was following up to dunk it back in. My jump shot was deadly, and I had range; you couldn't leave me open. I was about 6'3" by then and could handle the ball like a 5'9" point guard. I was sharp. But this came from all those days practicing in my back yard on Union Street. I can still visualize those days in my head, waking up early in the morning to shoot two hundred free throws and five hundred jump shots, waking up early in the morning to work on finishing with my left hand, waking up early in the morning to work on my ball handling skills. Waking up early in the morning to go run around the track with leg weights on and coming back home in lifting weights out in my barn. If I didn't have anything, I had some cement in the backyard, a basketball goal, a basketball, and a dream. I studied the game, I watched videos day in and day out. For years, I had done these things, day in and day out religiously. And someone was finally realizing my talents and wanted to give me the opportunity to grow them. That Myrtle Beach High School basketball head coach told my dad that if I was at their school that I would start as a guard on the varsity team alongside an already very well-known guard. My dad asked me what I wanted to do and the choice was obvious to me; this would keep my opportunity alive of getting a scholarship to go to college. So we made arrangements for me to stay with his friend and their family at the beach and go to Myrtle Beach High School my senior year. I appreciate Coach Buddy Rogers, who was the head coach at the time, for giving me an opportunity that year, and he has since passed away (he will forever be appreciated by me and my family). I was seventeen in 2003 when I left home and haven't been back to live there since I returned from out west in 2013.

I had a productive season my senior year at Myrtle Beach High School under this new system, averaging around 10 points, 10 rebounds a game, but it wasn't enough. My father made some sacrifices for me to have that opportunity and rooted in me the value of an opportunity. I still remember as the basketball season begin to play out, and I wasn't getting the touches that I needed to put up the points I needed to get the notice that I needed. The school already had a well-known player, and he hardly ever passed up the ball. My father would tell me after the game, "Jarrel, what did we come down here for? You got to put up more points than that." I understood that he had made a lot of sacrifices to get me there, financially and otherwise. I was determined to make the most of the opportunity.

One night, we had a game against North Myrtle Beach High School (and they had a 7-foot center and a good starting lineup), and I put up 17 points, 11 rebounds, and 2 steals. I caught a dunk off the rim of a missed layup (by that already-known player we had), and the very next play, I caught a fast break, beat one defender, and dunked it again, and their coach called a timeout. I couldn't miss that night from the 3-point line, it seemed like. After the game, my dad came down from the stands and hugged me, and that night, it all seemed worth it.

But at the end of that year, I didn't receive any scholarship offers to go to college and play basketball. But I did receive an academic scholarship offer for around $3,000 annually to go to South Carolina State University and an offer to become a preferred walk-on at South Carolina State University after meeting the coach and working out for him, so I went to SCSU of Orangeburg, South Carolina, to be a walk-on on the basketball team and further my education. This would at least keep the opportunity alive of one day becoming a professional athlete and moving my family out of our impoverished city. But coming into college, I had no one to show me the ropes. It wasn't as if my mother or father had been to college or received college degrees. How do these student loan things work? What is the interest? When do I have to pay them back? What is financial aid? What are grants, and do I have to pay them back also? How much is my tuition? Who do I need to talk to about these things? What should I major in? What classes do I need to take? What are prerequisites? Is it necessary that I go to this orientation thing? Do I qualify for any other scholarships because $3000 wasn't going to cover everything? What is a refund check, and do I get one? I had so many questions and *no* answers. I really didn't know where to begin, but I knew what my goals were, and I was willing to make it work by any means necessary. I ended up signing a bunch of papers for student loans and financial aid. I ended up gearing my major toward business because it was the only thing I was familiar with as I searched through my degree options. I didn't understand, in its entirety, what I was getting myself into. But anyway, I was in, and that's all that mattered to me. So I practiced with the South Carolina State University Bulldog basketball team for a year, getting prepared to make my debut the following year. I worked hard at practice and tried to show the coach every day that I deserved to be a scholarship athlete. Things seemed to be looking up. I was going to school and getting solid grades. And I would be contending in contested games for a pretty good Division 1AA school. I still had to make ends meet though. I needed gas for my car. I needed to feed myself outside of what I was getting at my family's house that I was staying with in Orangeburg, and I needed things for school as well. So I went back to one of my skills—I hustled. I sold on campus, to students, to people in the community I had met. So I was managing to get by. But lo and behold, that following year, the head coach that had brought me into the basketball program took another job coaching somewhere else. This meant that any player that wasn't on scholarship was immediately dropped from the team because the new coach would have his own preferred walk-ons and recruits that he would be bringing into the program. The players that were on athletic scholarships were already locked into binding agreements with SCSU and were secure. All seemed lost; if I wanted to walk-on with the new coach, I would have to reintroduce myself and try out again and possibly even sit out another year. But I was determined to keep hope alive. I believed in myself and my abilities. I knew what I had was rare, and I still had ambitions of buying that big house for my parents and retiring them and starting a solid foundation for me and my future family.

So I left SCSU and went to Clinton Junior College in Rockhill, South Carolina. I figured here I could redevelop myself in the world of college recruitment. But even at Clinton Junior College, I would have to walk on and prove myself as a player because the coach there wasn't aware of me or my talents. CJC was one of the few junior colleges in South Carolina with a basketball program. I was willing to take the risk, and I made the team as a walk-on and strived to prove myself to my new coaches. I sign some more papers to get some more loans. I was the only walk-on that made the team at CJC that year, but there were still the coach's recruited players ahead of me, so I would be working from the bottom again. The same problems I had while at SCSU I had at CJC. I still needed eating money and money for books and money for gas, so I hustled while at CJC. It was a small school and campus, so I took the whole school over. Since it was so small and they often had drug dogs come in and search the dorms, I hid my "work" nearby off campus. The basketball season was an all right one, but I didn't receive much playing time nor the notoriety that I wanted and was back at square one again. Twenty years old already and had no buzz in the basketball world. I had taken a step back and still nothing. What is my next move now? During these times, my father had little advice for me because I had ventured off into levels of basketball that he wasn't familiar with, and that was besides the fact that he and my mother were one generation from an outhouse (bathrooms used outside the house). He hadn't gone to college or played college basketball. Did I just have to give up on being a professional athlete? Should I have just tried my chances as a full-time drug dealer? Paying for and getting through school was hard enough; should I just have given up on getting an education all together?

The same friend that had gone with me on that trip to Highpoint, North Carolina, to meet my new connect was now staying out in Las Vegas, Nevada. I linked up with him and his family (the same friend of my father that I stayed with in Myrtle Beach). After talking it over with my father about the type of opportunities that were out there, I made the decision to move to Las Vegas to continue to pursue better opportunities. I got a one-way ticket to Las Vegas. I didn't have much money, just a hope and a dream. I got a job, and my friend and I got an apartment together. I was in hot pursuit of any and every opportunity I could get my hands on. I ran into hard times in Las Vegas as well. Times got rough there also; at one point, my friend and I were staying with three strippers we had met. For the time being, it was what I had to do; it was a roof over my head and food in my stomach. I was in a foreign place, but I still had ambitions of being a professional basketball player. So I and my father's longtime friend got up with the UNLV basketball coach and asked him if I could join his other players with their open gym runs at the school that summer. I told him that I did have some collegiate basketball experience already. He said yes. So I got up with one of the players and begin to start playing with them every day. Many of the players were impressed with my game. I told one of the already UNLV basketball players—we called him Tree—that I was interested in walking on, and his immediate response was, "For sure you will make the team easy, bro." I stood out at the open gyms there as I had before in other places. All of this was great, but still I didn't have the money to pay to go to school. I was already "up to my neck" in student loans. And this school was more expensive than SCSU to go to. It was a lost cause. So I continued to work and continued to search for other opportunities. I quickly learned that Las Vegas also had an inner city and impoverished areas in their city. Things were tight, even as I was working two jobs simultaneously. I would work at Armani Exchange during the day as a salesman and work at Neighborhood Wal-Mart overnight as a stocker. Still I struggled to make ends meet. One day, my car got towed, and the amount to get it out was ridiculously high. For two weeks, I was walked to work, both jobs. And my two jobs were miles and miles away from my apartment. But I continued to do what I had to do. I started hustling in Las Vegas as well, on the side, to coworkers and friends in the community I had met. A particular coworker I met introduced me to some of people she knew in the inner city, and I started selling to some of them as well. At times, I also sold clothes in Las Vegas. I remember one day when I was coming into one of the neighborhoods to make a sell. There was a policeman parked on the side of the road sitting in his car right as I approached the neighborhood. The policeman saw that I was in a nice car, a forest-green Cadillac Deville with a peanut ragtop on 22-inch chrome wheels, and started to tail me. My father had told me earlier in life when he began to teach me how to drive that as an African American in a nice-looking car, the police are bound to pull you over. He told me this for no other reason than what he had experienced in his own life as an African American driving in nice-looking cars and the proven history of the struggle of blacks in America. That policeman in Las Vegas that day followed me into the neighborhood without any probable cause. I hadn't broken any rules of the road. I had been through this before, at times when I was hustling and times when I wasn't. I knew I was fed up with it this day. That day in Las Vegas, I got into a brief high-speed chase with the police and I got away. He began to tail me as I was coming out of the neighborhood, so I turned back onto the block to see if he was really tailing me. He continued to follow me. I made a right; he made that same right, I made another right, and so did he. I made a right back onto the main street and made another right back onto the block and sped up a little bit to create some distance between me and him, but I could still see him in my review mirror, and he was still following me. I made another right and sped up some more, and now I was a whole Stop sign to Stop sign ahead of him. I made another right and quickly turned right down a tight alleyway right before the main street. He thought I had made another right back onto the main street, but I was in my car riding right beside him in the alley way parallel to him. I watched him as he looked around trying to see where I had gone. He was completely unaware that I was right beside him. So I threw my car in reverse and backed out the alleyway; he turned back onto the block thinking that I had turned back onto the block, and this time he put his sirens on. So I knew the chase was really on. I backed out the alleyway and turned back onto the main street and punched the gas on that V8. I got up to about 110 mph going down that main street, and by the time he had circled the block again I was already about two miles down the road and had made another right down another main street. I knew that they could call in for helicopters, and just driving fast wasn't going to get me away. I drove about another quarter mile down that street and parked my car on the side of a building that was a convenience store so that it wasn't visible from the main street. I got out of the car and started walking in the opposite direction of which I was driving. By this time, he had called in for backup, and he and another trailing patrol car, both lit up with sirens, passed right by me at a high speed as I was walking. They did not notice it was me who they were after, and I turned around and got back in my car. I drove off in the opposite direction they were going in, now doing the proper speed limit of course, and proceeded to go back home.

It was like no matter where I went, this was the life that was meant for me, no matter how hard I tried to do the opposite of what was wrong. It felt as if I was going against the grain. But isn't this the right thing to do? To try and pursue your dreams and your gifts in a society that preaches to us about the American Dream (Dream until your dreams come true), for America is the place structured for such talents (being that they are, in fact, talents) to blossom? This is the place that encourages higher learning and to try and get an education. If this is what they were telling us in school to do, then why was it so hard for me to do?

I had to do something. I was now twenty-two years old, and a professional basketball career wasn't manifesting. I was just in Las Vegas staying afloat. One day, one of my cousins on my mother's side of the family got in touch with me; he too was from the city that I was from, and he told me that he was out west in California now playing football at a junior college. He suggested that I give football a try; he and I were the same age. I had never played football in junior high or high school, much less college. I had little experience with the sport mentally or physically besides having tossed around a football a few times before. But I did my homework on it, and I saw that there were players in the NFL that had gotten late starts on their careers. There was a possibility that I could get picked up, although I would be in my mid-twenties before getting out of school. I knew I was athletic but wasn't sure where I would fit in at with the sport. But what I did know was that it was an opportunity, and if I made it work, I could buy my parents that big house and retire them and build a solid future for myself.

I was in a relationship by this time, so I and my girlfriend left Las Vegas and moved to Stockton, California, so I could play football at San Joaquin Delta College alongside my cousin. Since this was a junior college, my financial aid and a small loan would cover the tuition. I quit my job and drove out to California in my car to find a place to stay. The trip was by far not a short one. And I did not stop to get a hotel room because money was tight. I had trouble trying to find a place out there and was sleeping in my car at night on the side of the road because money was tight. My cousin didn't have himself established there at the time either. And the school year would be approaching soon, and my lease in Las Vegas was about to end very soon. So I left my car and flew back to Las Vegas from Stockton, California, rented a U-Haul truck, packed my things, and drove out to Stockton, California, from Las Vegas, Nevada, again. I got back to Stockton, California, and was still having trouble finding a spot to stay. Here I was in another foreign place with no resources, little money, no home, and no job. I was homeless, looking for a place to stay during the day and sleeping on the side of road in my car at night. SJDC was open for summer classes, and I and my girlfriend would go to the school in the morning to use their facilities to wash ourselves. Here I was taking risks again, and this time I had someone with me that was depending on me as well. I knew I was built for these type of things, but wasn't sure if my girlfriend could endure them. For about a month, I was homeless, but we ended up finding a place to stay right before the school year started that we could afford with the money we had. It was an apartment in the hood, but we had a roof over our heads finally. It was a pretty rough neighborhood. My first day there I woke up to find that someone had attempted to steal my rims off my car that night.

I and my girlfriend eventually broke up, and I met a girl that was from that neighborhood; she really introduced me to the streets of Stockton, California. I started hustling to once again help make ends meet. I had found a job also, so now I was going to school, working, hustling, and playing football and trying to keep all these things going at a consistently high level. School required and demanded a lot of effort and attention. Work required and demanded a lot of effort and attention. And football required and demanded even more effort and attention. I was new to the game of football, and I wasn't sure where I would fit in.

One of the coaches suggested that I play linebacker on defense. I was naturally strong and athletic. I ended up sitting out a year and practicing with the team to learn the position and put on some more weight. I worked hard and learned the new position. I found that football was fun as well. I wasn't playing basketball, but I was enjoying being an athlete again. The following year came around, and I was 6'3", 240 lbs. solid. I was already fast and quick, but now my weight and strength was up. I had my bench press up to 375 lbs. My coach put me in the starting lineup that season, and I put up great numbers. I had 5 quarterback sacks, 65 total tackles, and 10 quarterback hurries. My speed and my agility I acquired from playing basketball all those years plus my natural athletic ability and my size and strength gave me a dynamic edge over the competition. I wasn't your typical football player. By now I didn't have any more eligibility to play on the Division 1 level, but I still could play for a Division 2 university. I saw that players did make it to the NFL out of Division 2 schools; the chances were slim but I stayed in pursuit. After that season, I sent my film out to many Division 2 schools and started to get calls and scholarship offers. Up until this point, I had never been offered a scholarship to play for a university. I was ecstatic. I ended up talking with the linebacker coach for Central Washington University. We arranged a visit to the school, and I drove out to Ellensburg, Washington, to Central Washington University from Stockton, California, that following summer to visit the school and talk with the linebacker coach. The coach was immediately impressed with my size and the film he saw. About two days after the visit, he called back and said, "We want you." I was already twenty-four by now and knew that I had to start putting a rush on things.

A few months later, I left my job, packed up my car, and began my road trip back to Ellensburg, Washington. I acquired two AA degrees from SJDC, both of which were interdisciplinary degrees, one in elementary education teacher preparation and the other in liberal arts and humanities.

The trip wasn't an easy one. These roads seemed deserted like the ones on the trip from Las Vegas to Stockton. It was winter during this time. My car started to run hot on me along the way. It got to the point where I was pulling over on the side of the road every twenty minutes just as I was approaching the state line in Washington. I used snow and ice from off the side of the highway to help keep the car's engine cool. I didn't have insurance on it, and I didn't have money to get it fixed. So I did what I had to do. I drove some until it ran hot again and stopped to let it cool off again and repeated the process. I was on the side of the road for thirty minutes at a time to let the car cool down. But I didn't let that stop me.

One thing for sure I had learned up until this point in life, through all my struggles, through all my failures, and through all my obstacles, was that opportunities are far and in between. They don't come around often, and sometimes they never show up. I had an opportunity and nothing was going to stop me from seizing it. I got my car to Ellensburg, Washington. I got to Central Washington University and immediately started working hard. I was refreshed and as ready as I had ever been. I saw the competition around me, and I knew what the competition looked like out in the collegiate football world. I figured I would come in and immediately start. I would have a great season and could enter in the NFL draft by twenty-five years old with a solid university to back me.

From when I got to Central Washington University until when I left, nobody outworked me on the field or off the field. From when I got to CWU, I stood out amongst the competition. I was humbled with coaches and showed the willingness to continuously learn. The linebacker coach that recruited me to the school ended up leaving about a month after I got there, but I was still in the program. But this left me with other coaches that were still not very familiar with me. But I continued to work hard and show my willingness to learn. I only played in one game my junior season at CWU despite the fact that I was by far better than the other linebackers and defensive ends around me. It was like they wanted me to prove myself to them as if I owed them something or that I should have appreciated just being on the team. But I knew I had put the work in and deserved to be playing. I never missed a practice, was on time, and went to class as I should. There were only a handful of African American players on the team, and I noticed that they treated the other African American players the same way. There were other African American players that had been in the program before me that weren't getting any playing time as well and ones that I felt deserved to be playing as well. I was patient my whole junior season, but I observed what was going on around me. Ellensburg, Washington, is a predominantly Caucasian (white) town with about 90 percent of the town being Caucasian, and Central Washington University was a predominantly Caucasian university. I had "Mrs. Midgleys" as professors now, and there were a lot of "Mrs. Midgleys" in the community when I went out to go grocery shopping, to the post office, etc. Here I was right before my opportunity, and it wasn't my work ethic, my ability, my humbleness, my attitude, my drive, my motivation, or my academics that were keeping me from embracing my goals. I had worked too hard, I had made too many sacrifices, and I had taken too many risks to get this far and let my opportunity pass before me. I decided to write a letter that ended up being four to five pages long to the president of CWU and to every person in high authority at CWU on the circumstances that I and other players like me were enduring and demanded that something be done about it; if not, I would be taking this issue outside the university for others to hear about it.

A Chapter within the Chapter

My Letter to the President

To whom it may concern,

I am writing this letter on November 10, 2011, to reach out to whoever is willing to listen to me and take action to rectify these wrongdoings about the unnecessary circumstances which I and many other African American football players have endured here at Central Washington University (CWU) from the coaching staff of the 2011 Central Washington University football team during this 2011 football season. The circumstances in which I am referring to consist of many acts, throughout the 2011 season, of blatant and underline racism directed toward African American players on the football team. These acts have ranged from saying racist remarks (blatantly and underlined) to being biased in favor of Caucasian players over African American players because of skin color. I myself witnessed and was a victim of both the abovementioned acts of racism because of me being an African American. I have stayed in many cities and states throughout the United States and have experienced acts of racism in almost all the places I have lived, so when it comes to understanding/acknowledging/being cognizant of racism, I am not naïve. I came to Central Washington University to be a student athlete with high hopes that I would receive an equal/fair opportunity to complete my degree and also an equal/fair opportunity to display my talents in a Central Washington University's football uniform on the field. This was not the case on the football field this year. Every day since I have moved here to Ellensburg, Washington, I have received stares and glaring looks from other students in class, on campus, etc., for no particular reason, but I haven't let that stop me from pursing my education in this very uncomfortable environment. Ellensburg, Washington, is a town that has racial makeup of the following: 88.07 percent white or Caucasian, 1.17 percent black or African American, 0.95 percent Native American, 4.09 percent Asian, 0.16 percent Pacific Islander, 2.86 percent from other races, 2.69 percent from two or more races, and 6.33 percent of the population Hispanic or Latino of any race. It seems almost normal for some Caucasians to open/blatantly express how they feel about other races with no consequence. I have been out here for going on a year now and have endured this uncomfortable environment while attending school but never expected to receive racism from the coaching staff. After experiencing this, it has made me even consider dropping out of school, and my grades have continuously dropped. The only reason I am writing this letter is I have reached a boiling point with not only the racism here in Ellensburg, Washington, but most importantly, the racism on the football team between coaches and players, which is completely inacceptable. It struck me as unbelievable that this could go on in a program where parents entrust their children with these same coaches. These are the coaches that are expected to be honest, fair, and trustworthy individuals but are completely the opposite. I think my worst fear is for these coaches to continue to run this football program and for other African Americans coming here in the future to join Central Washington University's football team and experience the racism/discrimination I have experienced. As a proud American, I honestly thought that living in the twenty-first century, we Americans would be above/past situations like this. Giving our unfortunate history of slavery and discrimination in America, we should now understand that we cannot grow as a nation supporting racism. I understand that all Caucasians are not racist as well as every coach isn't racist, but for the other coaches to see this happen and not say anything, they are just as guilty, which would be the entire staff. Pennsylvania State University's board of trustees just recently fired both Joe Paterno, Pennsylvania State University's legendary head football coach, and school president, Graham Spanier, for knowing about alleged child sex abuse between Jerry Sandusky, Paterno's former assistant, and eight boys while in their midst, throughout the years. Although Joe Paterno and Graham Spanier did not commit the alleged crime, they were still held accountable because of their awareness of the matter. If Pennsylvania State University is not above justly handling these unnecessary issues, then surely Central Washington University isn't.

Due to the internal conflict/racial tension derived from the racist ways of the coaches and racism ignored by other coaches and racism supported by many of the players on the team, the season was a disaster. The first game of the season was against Texas A&M Kingsville. We lost, marking CWU's second consecutive season opener dropped/lost against a nationally ranked opponent, also falling to Minnesota Duluth at home in last year's debut. We lost the second game, marking the first time since 1999 that CWU's football team had dropped their two opening games. Then we lost the third game of the season, marking the first time since 1980 that CWU has dropped its three opening games of a football season. We, at the time 0–2 in the conference, also saw a fourteen-game series winning streak against Western Oregon snapped, marking the Wildcats' first loss to the Wolves since a 14–2 defeat on October 20, 2001, in Monmouth, Oregon. On October 15, 2011, we, CWU 2011 football team, played Humboldt State University's football team at home and lost, marking the last home loss in a conference game since 2007, when CWU capped a two-year football stay in the now-defunct North Central Conference. The loss was the first-ever home defeat for CWU in a Great Northwest Athletic Conference game, snapping a twenty-one-game streak since the league's inception in 2001. The defeat also marked the second time in the past twelve years that Central Washington lost on homecoming weekend. We currently have a record of three wins and six losses. With our last loss being to Simon Frasier University in Canada, the loss dropped us to a record to 3–6 overall and 3–4 in Great Northwest Athletic Conference play, assuring the program of its first below-.500 season since 2001. These records make this season one of the worst seasons in Central Washington University football history, with a game still up for grabs in the season. The outcome of this historically bad season is factual proof that something went totally wrong this season internally. Before the season started, I can recall a past football player stating that this year's team was composed of the most African Americans he had seen since him being here at CWU, which was three years. I truly believe that this was precisely why many of the Caucasian players and some coaches just could not conceal their racist ways and true feelings toward African Americans on the team.

Coach Joe Lorig, assistant head coach/defensive coordinator/linebacker coach, was the most blatant coach in expressing racist/derogatory/discriminatory acts toward African American players on the team. It was circulated by word of mouth that Coach Joe Lorig openly expressed himself while in a position meeting this year about how he truly felt about African Americans as people/human beings, saying that and I quote, "My favorite players in the NFL are black, but I just don't like them as people." The comment was said to be followed by no laughter as if it were a joke nor was it taken back and apologized for later. The comment was heard by the majority of the linebacker core but was not spoken out about its existence to anyone of authority until now. Coach Joe Lorig, throughout the season, showed dislike for African American players in many ways, ways that include: looking at African American players in complete disgust when doing the slightest things wrong on the field and calling African American players "f**king idiots" when not meeting his approval on the field (only directed toward African American players). It was said that while traveling to Canada this year, an African American player was not moving through the security at a rate in which Coach Joe Lorig wanted him to, so Coach Joe Lorig looked back at Coach John Gariano (defensive line coach) and said, "Only one more week to deal with them." The word *them* could have been loosely interpreted, but with many players being familiar with Coach Joe Lorig's motives and personality, it was clear what the word *them* was referring to; it was referring to the African American players. It was clear in many positions on the team where some African Americans should have played over some Caucasian players but was completely overlooked, and many of the African American players believed it to be because of skin color. Yes, some African American players did play and even started this year on the field, but these were all the positions that African Americans are typically known to be good at, which were speed positions like corner back, running back, safety, and receiver. I feel that what is right/honest/just is that the best players should play given that they comply with the coaches/school/football program rules and put in the time asked of the coaches, whether that be on the field or in the weight room or in the classroom. In the linebacker core, which Coach Joe Lorig coaches directly, there were Caucasian players that noticeably made many errors but still played the majority of the season, even starting the majority of the season thus far. Coach Joe Lorig continuously coached up the Caucasian players through their errors on the field and shunned the African American players when we made some of those same errors. The same was said to happen with the defensive line core in which Coach John Gariano coaches; players were shunned despite their athletic ability, and they often just left African American players to learn and coach themselves through their errors. The same was said to happen on the offensive line which Coach John Picha coached. The same was said to happen at many other position groups which Coach Blaine Bennett was head of. It has circulated that in Texas this year for an away game while at a Texas restaurant having dinner, racist words were spoken by a Caucasian player to another Caucasian player. At the restaurant, for entertainment, there was a small band going from table to table playing music, and then the band got to a table where predominantly African American players were sitting, and the African American players sitting there started to clap with the band, just enjoying themselves in the fun-filled environment. The Caucasian player looked over to the other Caucasian player and said, "We can't take them anywhere." I think it is pretty obvious what was meant by this statement. This was the case many times this year, where some of the Caucasian players spoke freely about how they felt about the African American players on the team. So freely, in fact, that they said things like this around the coaches and even said things like this in conversations with the coaches. It was made clear from some of the Caucasian players on the team that they did not approve of hip-hip/rap music, music that was a large part of African American culture. Now it is anyone's right to approve what music they favor and don't favor. But almost every time a hip-hop/rap song would be played for pregame warm-up, it was expressed by many Caucasian players and some coaches that they were in complete disapproval of it. They would say things out loud like "All music isn't real music" and "This is the worst pregame music ever." They have the right to vocally express themselves however they want, but I say what is really the purpose of blatantly expressing this, expressing it so blatantly that it makes others around you hearing these remarks uncomfortable? Even when in the locker room, when African American players played hip-hop/rap music, Caucasian players would put on other music to drown it out. But when the situation was reversed and Caucasian players were playing the music they preferred, no one tried to put other music on to try to drown out what they were listening to. With the season turning out the way it is, many Caucasian players quickly pointed the "finger of blame" at the African American players indirectly, saying that we were the blame for the outcome of this season, but nothing like this was expressed amongst the African American players. I have witnessed numerous times where the African American players would try to embrace other Caucasian players, only to have those same Caucasian players say derogatory things about them behind their backs. These and numerous other acts of racism, blatantly and underlined, happened consistently throughout the year with no consequence.

I chose to remain anonymous in writing this letter for fear that I will not receive a fair/equal opportunity to complete my degree here at Central Washington University and/or continue to play football here at Central Washington University. This letter will go to many people of authority. This is a cry for action, action to make just this injustice. I will continue to bring cognizance to these matters here at Central Washington University within the football program until action has taken place. These coaches can dictate someone's future by giving that player a fair/equal opportunity or not. Lives can be changed forever

> according to whether a coach is racist and/or biased toward a certain group of players. I didn't come here to Central Washington University to say, "What if I had gotten that opportunity?" I came here to say, "Central Washington University gave me my opportunity (in the classroom and on the field), and I determined what came from it."
>
> —Anonymous student athlete

The school held an investigation on the issue and interviewed players and coaches randomly with "equal opportunity authorities." I was never interviewed. That following year, my senior season, the defensive coordinator resigned (and soon later the head coach would resign). They hired an African American defensive coordinator. I played defense, and the new defensive coordinator was very impressed with my performance on the field; he immediately worked me into the starting lineup. He was not biased to the color of the players; he seemed to play who deserved to be in that position. Just as it wasn't until I was a senior in high school that I had started on the varsity team, I was hoping that it wasn't too late, that it wasn't until I was a senior that I would start at this university. But just as I had been a senior in high school and I was now a senior at this university, I was determined to make the most of the opportunity. I ended up that season with great stats and was ranked fifteenth in the nation for forced fumbles according to www.NCAA.com, and during the season, I was ranked as high as second in the nation for forced fumbles. I had accumulated a good number of highlights during my senior year and was only four classes away from getting my degree despite the odds. But I wasn't going to be able to pay for school that next semester; I was out of personal funds and my scholarship and financial aid didn't cover all my tuition. I had just recently asked for some money from an old friend from SJDC's dad (might I add that he was white and was one of the very rare white people I had met along the way that was an all right human being) to pay on some money I had already owed to the school. I had to make a decision. I decided to drop out of school (and finish at a later date) and train for my pro day, an event that CWU hosted every year where NFL scouts could come out to see what talent would be coming out of that school that year and the NFL Regional Combine that I had plans to participate in, in Seattle, Washington. I was still determined to go all the way with this. But I had no money. The lease on my apartment was about to expire. I had to make a move. I still had the car I had driven out to Ellensburg, Washington, in, but I hadn't gotten it fixed, and it had just been sitting. I posted the car on Craigslist and waited. I had hit some really hard times around this time again. I wasn't going to school anymore, money was tight so I wasn't eating like I should, I was losing weight, and I was all out of options. I had been hustling off and on campus, but the money was slow. How was I going to keep this dream alive?

About two weeks later, after posting my car on Craigslist, a pimp from Seattle, Washington, called me about it. He asked about the car. I told him it had been sitting for a while, and I left it at that. We arranged to meet at a hotel to do the exchange. I was asking $1,500 for the car as is. When I got to the hotel with the car, I knocked on the hotel room door he was in. When he answered the door, he tried to rush and get out, but I caught a glance of a woman counting money on the bed in the room. He tried to give me $1,200 for the car and we ended up reaching an agreement of $1,250. Although I knew he had more money, he was taking the car as is. I took the money and began to walk down a nearby train track toward the city limits of Ellensburg, Washington.

Walking down those train tracks, I called my friend that was in Las Vegas and asked him if I could go to live out in Las Vegas with him for a while, while I trained for my pro day and NFL Regional Combine. So I used the money to book me a flight, and I headed back to Las Vegas, Nevada, and begin training at Phillipi Sports Institute. I was underweight and had to get back in shape, but like always, I was willing to put the work in. I trained hard and got my weight back up, I got my strength back up, and I got my wind back right. I trained day in day out for three months with some elite athletes and trainers and top-of-the-line workouts. (I actually trained on a daily basis alongside a fellow linebacker, a Samoan guy, from UNLV, who was entering the draft that year also and actually got signed as a free agent with the Seattle Seahawks that year.) I managed to pay for all my training, flights, and hotel rooms (by selling off some of my valuables) while trying to get myself in front of the right people at these events. The month of March 2013, I did a lot of flying. I flew from Las Vegas to Seattle, Washington, and caught a shuttle bus to Ellensburg. From Ellensburg, I caught the shuttle bus back to Seattle and flew back to Las Vegas and from Las Vegas back to Seattle again and from Seattle back to Las Vegas and from Las Vegas to Raleigh, North Carolina, and from Raleigh to Florence, South Carolina, when it was all said and done.

I showed up to my pro day ready. I weighed in at 235 lbs. and had great body measurements—long arms, big hands, a tall frame, all legs, and a stocked upper body. I did twenty-one reps with 225 lbs. on the bench press. I ran a 4.7 forty-yard dash in an inside facility on a hand clock and slippery flooring. A fellow teammate that participated that day also ran a 4.7, but he played defensive back and only weighed about 175 lbs., to give you an adequate comparison. The Seattle Seahawks had representatives at the pro day that day. I showed up to the NFL Regional Combine that month also and hosted at the Seattle Seahawks Training Facility. There I had a great workout also. My workout was so good, in fact, that I was selected following my workout from over two hundred defensive players in attendance to do an interview with the Q13 Fox News. After the workout, they had everyone go into an auditorium for a Navy/Army presentation, but before they started, they said they needed to see about six or seven players out front. They started to call names, and I had my ears pitched because I knew that these were the players that they saw stand out in the workout. After about the third name, I heard the man say "Jarrel Johnson," and I jumped out my seat and headed out front. Here I was, a guy from a small impoverished town standing before cameras at a major event. I was once again ecstatic and "cheesing" (smiling uncontrollably) during my interview. No words could express how I felt walking back to the hotel that day. I had two great workouts under my belt. I had accumulated great college film highlights. I was ranked fifteenth in the nation for forced fumbles according to www.NCAA.com. I had played in Texas, Utah, Canada, California, Oregon, Washington, and stood out, so people knew about me. I had been a scholarship student athlete at a decent university, and I was soon to sign agent representation with a certified agent of the NFLPA. But I was broke again. I had invested everything I had; I had given all I could give (hustle, finances, time, everything), but I had run my course. I had nothing to do now but wait and see if the fruits of my labor would come to pass. The only problem with that was it was now out of my hands and I would have to hope that through all this, someone would give me a real opportunity.

CHAPTER 4

Going Back Home

I borrowed some money from my sister and my grandmother and booked a one-way flight back to Bennettsville, South Carolina, to be with my family when the news came through.

I watched the entire NFL draft that year from start to finish. I didn't hear my name get called. I waited weeks after the NFL draft, hoping that my agent would call and say, "Such-and-such team wants you to come to their minicamp and give you a tryout." But no call came through. Months went by, and it started to set in that I wasn't going to get a call from the NFL. But the guy that I had trained alongside at Phillip Sports Institute from UNLV got his call, as I mentioned before. I had worked out with him for months, so I knew that I was bigger, stronger, faster, and more athletic than him (nothing against him, but he wasn't even close to the athlete I was), but when he got his call and I didn't, I still texted him to tell congratulations. I realized that the risk hadn't worked. I had invested all my time (years I spent), money (I had accumulated huge amounts of debt), and effort (relentless amounts of energy) into this one risk this one opportunity. I had risked it all, everything I had what little I had and here I was back in Bennettsville, South Carolina again with no car, no money, no job, and no career.

I say "lol" because through all these risks, life experiences, sacrifices I had made, and decisions I had made, I had truly mastered the art of "bouncing back." Along my journey, I would let nothing stop me. Making something out of nothing is why I could tell someone that you still have another option, that there is always an option. I have started from the bottom so many times, over and over again, that surviving and thriving has become a skill. It is from my life experiences that I could coach someone through their life. It is from my business in the streets to my businesses online to my many entrepreneur endeavors that I could advise you in your business. It is from my struggles that I could tell you what success truly means. It is from my work ethic that I could tell someone what it truly means to have a work ethic. From hustling as a black man in America, I could truly tell someone what it means to hustle against the odds. I had let nothing stand in my way; I had made no excuses, so I can tell you when you have an excuse hidden in your path. It is from my drive that I could tell you what having drive truly means. It is through my motivation that I could motivate another when all seemed lost. It is through my will that I could tell one what having will truly means.

When I got back to Bennettsville, South Carolina, in 2013, I was completely out of money but hopeful. I was hopeful that I would get some sort of call from the NFL. I was completely confident of myself and hopeful, hope that wasn't farfetched. As I mentioned before, I was a proven player. I had put myself out there and performed at every event. The draft went by, and so did the months, and no one called. I did some CFL workouts and still nothing. There I was back where it all started with nothing—no resources, no money, and no job. So I started hustling anything I could get my hands on, and it was enough to keep food in my mouth and stay out of my family's pocket. All those years I had been gone, I had seen many people I grew up with make no substantial growth in their life and some none at all. I met the woman who is now my wife and daughter's mother. We moved in together because I felt that she was sincere for taking a chance with me despite me not having much at the time, and we got close.

I was without a job for about a year. Then I finally got a job in my hometown and became permanent, thanks to a caring family member already working there, and I stopped hustling, but not for my old lady or my job but because I found out that an informant had given the police some information on me and I was under investigation. I became very good at my job as a forklift operator; I quickly learned how to drive and operate every forklift in the factory. Even as a forklift operator, I was shining. I could operate multiple forklifts facing forward or facing backward. The head man of our department (a white man) couldn't help but come out of his office to make himself be known. He would get on forklifts and drive them through the warehouse for no apparent reason (I guess to show me that he also could drive them but without the grace that I could drive them with), and when that wasn't enough, he would walk through the warehouse and walk out in front of my forklift.

One day, I was driving my forklift, and he walked past me and then quickly turned back around in front of my forklift, and I almost hit him. He said, "You better not hit me with that forklift" as if he was completely unaware that he was in the wrong in that situation. He was looking for some type of submissiveness from me, and I knew it, but just as I didn't play that role when I was trying to earn a spot on the field or on the court, I wasn't going to play that role in that factory driving forklifts. These were the same things I had experienced in life as a child and a teen before I left to go out west. And the same thing I had seen going on in other areas in life I had experienced out west was happening in this factory here in my hometown as well (now as an adult). No matter where I was located at in this country, what city I was in, what state I was in, whether I was in school, whether I was in a factory, whether I was playing basketball, or whether I was playing football, this was the name of the game. So if this was the name of the game, then the blacks in the game and those willing to play along with the game had to be ones that were allowed to survive and thrive in the game. I looked up to Michael Jordan, and he was a world-class athlete, no doubt, but Jordan was not alone in his world-class athleticism. And for every Michael Jordan that made it in the game, there are other Michael Jordan's that have not made it in the game. There was a black guy that had been working in that factory for about twenty years, and he was the epitome of an Uncle Tom. Every time the head man (that same white man that would walk out in front of my forklift) walked in, in the morning, he would run up to him and speak and laugh at all his jokes and laugh even when he didn't make a joke. I couldn't believe it, because this was the same guy that was working back in the warehouse with me that would act like he didn't like me for any apparent reason. Just as I had seen players play for being Uncle Toms, I saw this man benefit in life through his job for being an Uncle Tom. I worked for a few months, and my now-wife got pregnant. Shortly after finding out she was pregnant, out of nowhere, I got a call from the director of player personnel for the Columbus Lions of the Professional Indoor Football League.

Coach Banner, director of player personnel, contacted me in November of 2014 about the opportunity to earn a one-year contract to play with the Columbus Lions of Columbus, Georgia. At the time, I was twenty-eight years old and working as a forklift operator at Marley Engineered Products in Bennettsville, South Carolina, in my hometown. My job was permanent, I had a daughter on the way to be born in just a couple of months (my first child), and I was engaged to be married to the mother of my child. I was somewhat settled in back in South Carolina. Until Coach Banner had contacted me, my dreams of being a professional athlete had seemed like a lost cause. Coach Banner and I talked on the telephone back and forth for a few days discussing the opportunity, and then one day on the phone, he told me, "These opportunities only come around once in a lifetime." The opportunity was a great opportunity; in fact, the Columbus Lions as an organization advanced 25 percent of their players annually to better football leagues such as the NFL and the CFL. It was what I needed to hear to get myself in gear. He told me that in a month they would be holding a tryout in Columbus, Georgia, and that this would be the time for me to show up and show what I had to offer. I was a little disappointed that after all I had already accomplished as a football player (I had played and started on the San Joaquin Delta College football team; earned an athletic scholarship to play at Central Washington University, concluding my senior season at Central Washington University; was ranked fifteenth in the nation for forced fumbles; displayed my talents across the nation and out of the country; and participated in the NFL Regional Combine in Seattle, Washington, where I was selected after my workout to do an interview with the Q13 Fox News; trained at world-class facilities and with world-class athletes; and played alongside world-class athletes as well) I would still have to prove myself. But this was something that I was now no stranger to. Although my fiancée and I both worked, we still lived paycheck to paycheck, and money was tight. Just making this workout would be a stretch for me financially. I would have to purchase my own shoulder pads and helmet; pay for gas for the round trip from Bennettsville, South Carolina, to Columbus, Georgia; feed and house myself along the way; and take the time off from work to do so. That was just the financial side of things. I would also have to get in shape for the workout while still going to work every day and maintaining my everyday life. I was underweight, not as strong as once was, and nowhere near good running condition. I had a month to put everything together, and I did. I put on about ten more pounds and scrapped up a few dollars to make the trip happen. The workout was supposed to be a two-day event, but concluding my first day of working out for the team, Coach Banner let me know that I had an official invitation to the Columbus Lions minicamp coming that March 21, 2015. I was back; I felt rejuvenated. It was a great accomplishment, for only 0.08 percent of college athletes go on to play professional sports of any kind.

CHAPTER 5

Not Another Risk

I came back after the workout and the great news, and shortly after, my baby girl was born, Leeona Johnson. She was born on January 27, 2015, at 7:30 p.m., weighing 6 lbs. and 2 oz., was 19 inches long, and was every bit of her father. She is the overall reason that I am writing this book, to promote a healthy society and a better world for her sake. She will be gifted also (the signs are already showing), and I would hate for her to not flourish as she should because the society she lives in prevents it. Playing professional football for the Columbus Lions of the Professional Indoor Football League was a great opportunity, but it still was a risk I would be taking. I would be risking losing a job, my fiancée losing her job, giving up the home we were settled in and renting, money invested—risking it all again just for the opportunity. Up until this point in my life, I had risked it all, but not with a child I was responsible for involved. I had slept in cars alongside deserted highways, gone days without eating, stood in lines at food banks to get groceries, all in pursuit of an opportunity, but never would I have done something like that with a child involved. I wanted to make sure that this would be something that I really wanted to do. I was sure of my athletic ability and what I could bring to the organization as a player and a person, but I had been sure of all these things in the past and still there was unnecessary turmoil, unnecessary discrimination, unnecessary circumstances placed around me, just unnecessary events I had no control over. But the opportunity to create a better life for my family than I had overrode everything I could possibly think of. I had three months to get ready for the move; there was so much I had to do. I would have to relocate me and my family six hundred miles, relocate two cars, relocate all our belongings and furniture, and get the money to do so. Not to mention my daughter was to be born about a month from the time I got the invitation to minicamp. I would also need to continue to get ready physically for minicamp if I wanted to show up ready and earn the one-year contract. Thinking back on all I did to make the move happen, it hurts to type it all now.

My grandmother had recently passed, and she had believed dearly in my athletic career. She had even given me money to make some previous workouts for other teams in the past (after returning from out west in 2013). She had died from cancer, and I really wanted to do it not only for my family but for her, in her honor. My grandmother knew I was a champion, a champion without opportunity, a champion that the "system" had neglected, a king denied his throne from appearance and systematic limitations, and she was willing to back that, back the family's champion. She knew if I made it, then everyone made it. She looked at me as a hero for the family, as if I could save us from the poverty and circumstances around us.

I had three months to get ready for the move. I keep working at my job, putting back what money I could to get ready for the move, but it was going to literally take thousands of dollars to relocate my family, me, and the life we had started in South Carolina to Columbus, Georgia. So I started hustling again, linking up with some old partners from California to get ready for the move. I couldn't see it happening any other way; the jobs we had were just giving us enough to stay afloat and pay the bills. I was back in my hometown area hustling, so I made way for a few people around me and some family in nearby cities to eat well too. I was putting a lot of people in position to make money as I made money myself. As the move got closer, I was back and forth from Bennettsville to Columbus trying to get life established in Columbus. I was in and out of different hotels in different cities, renting cars, etc., trying to make the leap, and time was steadily closing in fast. I was choreographing the move to Columbus, hustling, helping my fiancé with our newborn, maintaining life in South Carolina, and getting established in Georgia. It was time for us to make the trip, and we made it. I remember arriving in Columbus at around 1:00 a.m. in the morning with the U-Haul, a car being towed on the U-Haul, and my fiancée and daughter following in my car behind us. Already tired from an eight-hour commute, I didn't even rest at our new Loft apartment upon arrival. I immediately begin to unload the packed cars and the U-Haul. I didn't stop unloading until 6:00 a.m., and still I hadn't unpacked all our things.

Columbus was a nice city and full of potential and opportunity for us. I was enjoying playing alongside other accomplished collegiate graduates from across the nation; there were players from Duke University and players like me from the opposite side of the map. But once again, every day in practice, I stood out; no one that I saw could match my athletic ability. My coach handed me my playbook one day after practice, and I know once you get that playbook, you're in the game. And with some hard work, my weight and strength was back on the rise. I could take 325 lbs. off the rack on the bench press and bench it with no spot. But it was still like I was in a position to prove myself to the organization, and I was being stalled and not progressed. As I mentioned before, there was no better athlete that I could see on the team. New players were being brought in from across the nation as camp went on, but still no one showed up that was a better athlete than I was. I was covering all the bills until my wife got back on her feet and going to practice every day. And the only task my wife had was to take care of the newborn, who was about two months old now, which seemed to be an unusually difficult task for her, and she needed my assistance in that area despite me already having a full load. After a few months of this and dealing with her family telling her myths of me not actually playing football for the Columbus Lions, I ended up taking her and my daughter to one of my practices to prove to her that I was with the organization. That practice ended up being my last practice as a professional athlete, for by then, the weight had mounted up on me and I had to pull the plug a week before I was to suit up.

We came back to Bennettsville, South Carolina, leaving behind most of our belongings, including her vehicle as well because she had forgotten her keys back in South Carolina after returning to Columbus to retrieve what items we could take back with us. And on the way back to South Carolina from Columbus, we got pulled over in Augusta, Georgia. I was driving because my wife didn't travel well and wasn't familiar with the open road. I tried letting her drive for a few hours one time while going to Columbus from South Carolina while I got some rest, and when I woke up, we were almost in Montgomery, Alabama. But anyway, we got pulled over, and I had a suspended license, so I ended up getting locked up. I explained to her briefly how to get back home, and they hauled me in. I was released that morning in a city I knew nothing about and with no one to pick me up from the jail. I was given one phone call, and I called her to let her know that I was out and would need her to pick me up by the interstate where we were stopped by the police. The jail was very far off from the interstate, and I knew she wouldn't be able to find it, but the interstate was basically a straight shot from South Carolina once she got on it. The only problem with that was I didn't know how to get back to the interstate myself. I left the jail and went to a business and asked how to get to the I-20. It took her about three hours to get back to the exit where we had been stopped, and it took me that same amount of time to walk back to that exit off I-20. After all we had been through, it was still like she wasn't sure if I was completely for her, so even after all of this, I married her around this time. My father, now a pastor, married us in the living room of the house I had grown up in.

But now, once again, I was back in Bennettsville, South Carolina, with nothing, and this time, I had brought back home with me a wife and a baby on top of the fact that I had put a tremendous amount of effort and money into making that move and it had been in vain. I had to fight through some days of regret, regretting a lot of things. But after a few months of enduring, I got a call for a possible manager position in a retail business establishment, and I ended up getting the job and still have it to this day. Shortly after getting the job, I started hustling again. I had to get my family back on our feet, and although I was appreciative of the job, it wasn't enough. And just like times before, I was doing what I had to do. I bounced back; it was one of the major most important comebacks of my life because now all eyes were on me. People around me saw satisfaction in the fact that I and my family were down and out, and if they had anything to say or do about it, I would have stayed down and out (classic "crab in the bucket" mentality and Willie Lynch Syndrome). But since I had fallen off this last time coming back from Columbus, around one year ago from me writing this now, I have purchased three cars (I have four and own three of them) and moved my family into our own space with no credit, and did it all right before my wife finally found a job. This was proof once again (twice in person for my hometown since coming back in 2013 and a number of times before in general) that with some hustle, you can still succeed against the odds and create a better life, real opportunities, real growth for you and your family. Nothing to do with or about the system I live in here in America had to do anything with the last time I bounced back or any other times I did. And that is because the system is not structured for true greatness, the American Dream is not structured for true greatness.

CHAPTER 6

No Means Yes

Our children must know the real odds they face in life as they venture out into the world in pursuit of their dreams, full of false hope in a society full of unreal opportunity that has been pumped into them through forms of mass media by a corrupt system. I never took no for a final answer. I grew up seeing my father go to prison and still not taking no for a final answer. Even in prison, he continued to find loopholes and hustle. He even got a job while in prison, and we never missed a Christmas. And after getting out of prison, he continued to go against the odds and went into business for himself. He would never lie down, and I, being the seed of him, was bound to never lie down. I ran into many nos and experienced many failures. My father helped me fight through my first no involving the system, when I was denied being a varsity player in my hometown and we made the decision to relocate me to Myrtle Beach to start as a varsity player. We were not taking that no because he and I knew that I was far better than any other player my hometown or surrounding areas had to offer (which I ended up finding out for sure). We got through that first one together, and I took it from there. I could have stopped at SCSU when the head coach ended up taking another job somewhere else, but I didn't. I could have stopped at CJC when no college scholarship offers came through to continue to play college basketball. I could have stopped in Las Vegas. The city was full of infrastructure, I had job opportunities to join the workforce and make a living, and there was plenty to see and do. But I kept pursing the real opportunities of life, taking one major risk at a time. When I got to SJDC and I didn't understand the game of football, I could have given up. I could have accepted that "no" from CWU and just sat on the bench my senior collegiate year, but I didn't. I stood up for what was right, and I was right; I ended being a nationally ranked player in my division. If I had accepted that no, then I would have never achieved that. I never would have accomplished my goal of becoming a professional athlete if I had accepted any of those nos. Someone else was trying to control my destiny, and I stood up for myself. Don't accept no, don't accept a partial no, and always stand up for what's right. I was moved from the positions on the football field I wanted to play, and I adapted and still performed. I was willing to change cities and states if necessary, making moves with little to no money at times. Even now, as a manager, I go through daily obstacles at my job, and most are unnecessary. I could give up and quit, but what example would I be setting for my daughter? What example would I be setting for the future of black America? People come to my job with the most unnecessary things they can think of to try to provoke a reaction from me. But failure has never been acceptable, no matter the system or the situation. For me, no means yes, and wrong is right in many cases. If I hadn't looked at life in that way, then I would have never left my hometown in the beginning and thus have never left my mark on the world, a world that would have my greatness erased.

CHAPTER 7

A Journey for Opportunity and Traveling the World in the Process

From Bennettsville, South Carolina, my father would take me and my brother to Manhattan, New York. As a young man, that was fascinating to me. I and my brother became old enough to drive, and we would help make the trip. So in my teens, I became familiar with traveling. We would make stops in Virginia, Pennsylvania, New Jersey, and other states along the way. I remember one trip we stopped in New Jersey and saw Mike Tyson at a travel stop. It was an unreal experience. We were seeing all kind of things that weren't going on in Bennettsville. It was exposure and an opening of the mind. Once in Manhattan, it was all business; we hit the streets, and it was one store to the next. There were food stands alongside the walkways, and it seemed like everybody was selling something. There was a food stand that sold chicken and rice plates; that was the best chicken and rice I had ever tasted in my life. I can taste it right now as I write this portion of my autobiography. I have to go back one day and get me one of the chicken plates, preferably two plates, one being a to-go plate.

My senior year in high school, I moved to Myrtle Beach, South Carolina, in pursuit of an opportunity to start as a varsity basketball player. I ended up getting a job down there as well at Friendly's Restaurant on Ocean Boulevard. Myrtle Beach was an exciting city and a tourist attraction. I met a lot of people while staying there. Hotels, outlets, and stores were everywhere. Just walking the beach was relaxing, and until this day, I still go back there to do so.

From Myrtle Beach, my next stop was Orangeburg, South Carolina, where I resided with my dad's brother and his family while attending South Carolina State University. South Carolina State University neighbored Claflin University, and it was another campus that I would visit also. Orangeburg was a city centered around its universities. While attending SCSU, I met a lot of people from surrounding cities, and it was where I had my first experience as a college student.

From Orangeburg, I went to Rock Hill, South Carolina. Rock Hill wasn't too far from home, but it was still a different area. I made friends with most of the people who attended Clinton Junior College (Clinton was a very small school) with me and often visited their hometowns in Gaffney, South Carolina; Charleston, South Carolina; and Columbia, South Carolina. Charlotte, North Carolina, wasn't too far from Rock Hill, and we often visited the city to see what they had going on.

From Rock Hill, my next stop was a six-hour flight to Las Vegas, Nevada. We all know about Las Vegas, but to live there was a totally different experience than visiting for a weekend. Las Vegas's boulevard was a hundred times more fascinating than Myrtle Beach's boulevard. In Las Vegas, I got the chance to visit the University of Nevada in Las Vegas's campus and play in their basketball facilities, walk through beautifully structured casinos, and even play a round or two of the games, and as mentioned before, I trained at Phillipi Sports Institute for my pro day and NFL Regional Combine. Las Vegas was one of the more favorable places of all my stops. The city was full of infrastructure and opportunity. You could find a job with ease. I worked at about five or six jobs while staying there. And I wouldn't mind moving back there one day in the future.

From Las Vegas, I went to Stockton, California. California, the sunshine state, the golden state, was another one of my more favorable places to reside. I did everything in California; I was an athlete there, a 9-to-5 worker, a student, a resident, and a hustler.

I would often visit the university of the Pacific and watch some of their contested (men's and women's) basketball games. While staying in California, I visited Modesto, Sacramento, San Francisco, Weed, and other cities. In the words of Biggie Smalls, "I'm going going back back to Cali Cali" one day.

From California, I went to Ellensburg, Washington, driving through Oregon in the process. Ellensburg wasn't one of my most favorite places to reside; it was a cold place, it seemed, year round. While in Ellensburg, as a scholarship athlete, I got the chance to visit Oregon again, Texas, Utah, California again, and I left the country for the first time, traveling to Canada. Traveling to Canada was a wonderful experience. I got a passport for the first time and got to see what it was like to leave a country and enter another one. The lifestyle was different in Canada. People on the streets and shopping malls were from all nations. I got chance to compete as an athlete in Canada, walk the streets, and eat in restaurants alongside other Canadians.

From Ellensburg, it was to Seattle, Washington, and a flight back to Las Vegas. And from Las Vegas back to Raleigh, North Carolina, and from there to Florence, South Carolina, and finally back to Bennettsville, South Carolina. And since coming back home, I have resided in Cheraw, South Carolina; Society Hill, South Carolina; and Columbus, Georgia. Columbus would be another city that I wouldn't have minded residing in preferably while continuing to be a professional football player.

CHAPTER 8

Blessed with More, So I Gave Back a Lot

Growing up, I always had a natural crowd around me. People saw something in me—something they could grow from themselves. I was gifted in many things; you could tell by the way I walked that the "chi" was strong with me. I never minded sharing these things; my loyalty had no limits, although in most cases, it ended up in jealousy and envy. Coming into high school, I had friends and family around me that played basketball as well, so while working on my own game, I would also help them develop theirs. If it were up to me, we would all make it. But I never made it easy for them; I would never let them win a game on the court. They were not going to get better if I let them win. I dressed well and would often sell my clothes to others in the neighborhood, but of course, I would have another "flyer" outfit off to the side. But I never minded giving back. I wanted to see them fly as well. I drove in nice cars and had unique taste in style. But I sold my cars as well, sold my rims and other car equipment. It was nothing to me to do it again or sell a car just to get some rims for another car I had. Often I sold these things to close friends around me because I wanted to see them shine as well.

I remember back in the day (before I left to go out west) when I was hustling and I went to visit some friends of mine that were fellow go-getters in the city and saw that they had fallen off. I knew that it was possible to fall off, but I also knew that these guys were some real hustlers; they were twin brothers. I fronted them some work that day, and I never saw them fall off again until they ended up catching some prison time. But I have seen one of them since coming back home in a club one night, and as I understand it, they are doing just fine. We had a ball in the club that night, it was my birthday. I often assisted my friends and family and motivated them in things they were trying to pursue. If they wanted to be an athlete, then I showed them what it took to be a great athlete. I showed them how to network in that area to keep achieving growth and take it all the way. If they wanted to hustle, then I showed them how to hustle, how to stay disciplined, how to save, how to shop for the best deals, how to negotiate those deals, how to build up and keep clientele, I showed them all aspects of the game and how to stay on top of that game.

When I was staying out in California, a friend of mine had run into some iPhone 4s when they had first come out. His sister had stolen them off a delivery truck but had gotten caught for the crime and needed bail money to get out. He had several boxes of them and needed to get rid of them as soon as possible. I brought two, posted them on Craigslist, and sold them in no time. So I went back and got three and did the same thing and flipped them. So I went back and got four and flipped them. Then after a while he started to ask me who I was getting them for (and the first thought that came to my head was *What does it matter? Doesn't your sister need this bail money?* And I knew what time it was, jealousy and worried if I was going to come up came into the equation. So I grabbed my last few (telling him that I was getting them for some family back home) and flipped them, and that hustle was over. I also had turned one of my friends in California onto the hustle while I was flipping the phones, and he made some money as well. I took all the profit, which was about a thousand dollars (in about a week) and sent it to a friend I considered to be close to me back in South Carolina. He was supposed to take the money and start flipping some work down there, and he ended up messing up the money. I never even asked for it back, and even after coming back from out west, I went on a hustle run with him. It was in any area of life that I could contribute to helping anyone around me I would. As my sister began college, I helped her get through school by helping her financially at times when I could and helped her with her classes. By the time she got in college, I had done messed up in college so much that I could now tell her what she needed to do and not do. If they wanted to rap, then I showed them how to stay consistent, how to strategize in that game, how to draw an audience, and how to network in that game as well. I was an advocate supporter in what they were passionate about; it was never just about me.

I actually tried to arrange a group of hustlers and go-getters (this was before I left to go out west) consisting of my friends, people from the neighborhood, and family. The purpose was to join resources and come together for a common purpose, which was to come up and do something different that the generation before us didn't do. But as I mentioned before, jealousy and envy planted a firm wedge between us and the movement, and I am the last standing in that movement today. I swear some people can't hustle if you tell them the game. When I got back to Bennettsville in 2013, I had a natural clinging around me, and still I was giving back in what ways I could. When I started hustling again, I showed others how to make that money and how to move and avoid certain setbacks. And it was my plugs and resources that made a noticeable difference in us coming up and making real money. And I showed love in prices, love that I could have kept to myself. Also, when I got back home in 2013, my brother was living with my grandmother that has since passed, and he was not working or doing anything significant with his life. As I applied for jobs, I also applied for him. The first job he got hired to after me coming back in 2013 was a job that I had applied to for him. I actually filled out his application for him. Before I was married and even now as a married man, I told my wife that it was never just about me. Although I exposed her to things she had never saw, I showed her that dreams do come true with some persistent hustle. She had never witnessed a professional athlete practice until I took her to my last one. And she never witnessed someone able to get money and strategize the way I do until she met me. She had never resided out of the town she grew up in until she met me. I opened up a new world for her although it was me that she was witnessing as a professional athlete and me that she was witnessing making these strategic moves, and it was me that she was witnessing making that money; I still gave her what she (and I) wanted, a family. I married her despite her unnecessary actions in Columbus that ended up sending us back to Bennettsville to show her that it wasn't just about me. I was willing to show her again that I was all in for the cause. I was supportive for her growth as an individual as well. I encouraged her about advancing in her career and furthering her education. All of this giving back never seemed like enough, and as I write this, it seems that I will be alone at the mountaintop, me and my kids of course.

CHAPTER 9

The Streets Will Never Stop Testing You

When I first started hustling, there was only one purpose, and that was to pursue a better life than what I was seeing around me and that I had growing up myself. But in the streets, you will never be proven and always tested. Your life always hangs in the balance, and it will be hard to get sleep at times. You will get to network with others, but you will never know who's trying to "snake" you. Your own friends will get jealous of your coming up and make a dirty play on you. You have nobody but yourself. And like my great-grandfather, Daniel Johnson, told my grandfather and my grandfather told my dad and my dad told me, "Don't be anybody's fool. Don't even be your own fool." Sometimes it's good to trust yourself, and if you've got a bad feeling about a play you're about to make, then don't do it. Live to fight another day, as they say. If something isn't adding up for you, then don't do it. I always made smart plays. Other people in the street envied me for that because I wasn't getting caught up like them, but my money was adding up. And I didn't care too much about being liked; I was loyal to the ones who showed me loyalty. But even loyalty will go out the door when someone around you isn't winning like they think they should be or not winning quite like you are. So beware of the mood changes, and look out for the switch-up.

I knew how to move in and out of the game and catch certain seasons. I knew how to go in and out of hustles. When something wasn't looking good or money was drying up in one hustle, I would take all my money and put it into something valuable like a car so that I would have an asset that was mine that I could always cash out or sit on and wait for something else to open up. Sometimes it meant taking dirty money and putting it toward school, if that was where the next opportunity or move was. You had to have a plan, and you had to be smart. And you got to know how to move; the game is chess, not checkers.

When I caught wind that I had served an informant and the police had some information on me, all the information they had was inaccurate, and to this day, that penalty is still pending. I learned that the hard way coming back home and being out of the loop for so long. Everybody wasn't clean; in fact a lot of my city had turned informants, and that was now the name of the game if you wanted to play it. You couldn't even tell your old lady, any woman you're dealing with, or your momma all your moves. Know your numbers and know when you're winning; sometimes putting somebody else in a position to win can be a win for you as well. It's not all about greed; get your money on the back end if you have to. You've got to keep an edge on your competition, whether that means keeping better quality work or staying consistent with your clientele. Listen, pick that phone up when it rings, and tell them something. All that shining and always in the spotlight isn't for that game. If you're always at the club, on the block, on "front street," on the scene, that isn't good, and if you see somebody in the game doing that and they never get caught up, then don't deal with them. If you end up turning into an informant to keep hustling in the streets, then that game wasn't ever meant for you. You are in it for the lifestyle and not to really come up because an informant can only make moves that are cleared by the person he is reporting to first, and his moves are limited. That's besides the fact that they can "flip" you whenever they feel like it. You should find something that you are good at and do that the best you can. It's not necessarily about what you're selling but how, when, why, where, and to whom you are selling it. I have sold different kinds of illegal narcotics and some at the same time (with different ways to sell them, different prices, and different ways to handle them). Your grind and hustle should be taken as seriously as your life itself. And if you're not hustling to come up and come out winning, then what are you doing it for? You either can hustle or you can't.

My last few runs, before I moved to Georgia and after I came back from Georgia, were profitable in the thousands. In any place I have lived in, clearing a thousand dollars to the pocket was damn near impossible. I made those runs after that informant—might I add I know who he is (and he happens to be someone from the same neighborhood I grew up in)—had run my name to the police. It's how you move and who those movements involve; it was basic supply and demand multiplied by strategy. I had the proper connections; I had linked up with some old partners from out in California. California is notorious for having good work and different work in certain divisions of the game. Made in California and sold in South Carolina, that's a whole other region. Bingo, when you got something on the market that somebody else doesn't have, whether that be of better quality or different in general, that makes what you have rare. When you got something rare on the market, then you got something exclusive on the market. When you got something exclusive on the market, then you basically can set your own price. I just had to get the product to me, and I wasn't driving out there to get it, so we arranged to put it on the first flight out. I told my plug to wrap it up tight and say a prayer when it arrived. Risky business, my friends—I know some people who have gotten jammed up trying things like that. And they are going to hit you with a charge for every state that it came through. I was sending work to friends back in South Carolina from California myself when I was staying out there, and I got a package taken by the police. I called the company to see what had happened to it, and she had me hold for a while and then got back on the phone and said it had been seized by the police, and I hung up on her. Getting the work was a risk in itself, but that was just the first part of it. I had to turn that work into money. But anyway, I had a plug. As I mentioned before, just getting it was a risky task in itself; I had to keep switching up addresses from city to city because you know the police have got a job to do too. I had to be careful how I moved with the work, driving with it and where I was stashing it at. The "jack boys" (robbers) are watching too, looking and waiting for you to slip up. The police are waiting for you to slip, and playing fair isn't in their vocabulary. Follow the rules of the road when you are riding dirty. I had to keep a tight circle so when some information got into the wrong hands I could trace it back and know where it came from. My plays were big plays most of the time—one big risk and one big payoff—and took place out of town. I linked up with some family members that stayed in bigger cities, and in bigger cities, they had more money to spend. I dealt with a few partners from back in the day that stayed in my hometown, but informants were like a cold in the winter; every corner had one. But my circle was small, so I could monitor what was getting out and who was putting that information out. I keep the small circle in my city circulating (putting money in some of my friend's pocket) and at the same time using that money to pay the plug back. I used bank accounts to send the money to them. All the big plays out of town were mine to make. I can remember one night I was out of town in the city with about ten thousand dollars' worth of work on me in the middle of the night, trying to make a play, and of course, I had my Glock .40 Smith and Wesson pistol on me. My last runs grossed in the amount of about thirty-five thousand dollars to forty thousand dollars. That's a lot of moving, a lot of watching, a lot of paying attention, a lot of strategy, and a lot of "how, when, why, where, and to whom you are selling it," especially where I come from. I did all that while maintaining a forty-hour-a-week job (at the beginning of my last run until now) because I knew that game didn't last forever and that after I was done, my check would still be there. You got to have an exit plan, a backup plan. It's about the overall win, winning in life, and it's hard to do that in prison, and you can't win in life if you spend your life trying to please someone else. I don't want to seem like I'm glorifying doing what I did; remember I just wanted to play at being an athlete. If you think that, then you are part of the problem. I just wanted to be great and was willing to do that by any means necessary.

CHAPTER 10

The Game Ain't Fair

Growing up like I mentioned before my dad would often take me to the basketball courts and teach me what he had learned on the court. And sometimes those lessons were tough ones. I wouldn't be listening or showing an attitude, and he would take the ball and hit me in the chess with it. It was tough love. He would often ask me if this was something that I really wanted to pursue. I would say yes, and it was an honest response. I loved the game of basketball, I loved being an athlete, and I could feel within myself that I had a gift for being an athlete that was worth showing to the world. He would say, "Well, if you do, then you can't half-step with it—you are either all in or not in." One day, we went to the court to play one on one, and I said to myself, "Yeah, this is the day that you hand that crown over to me" because I knew I had gotten better than him. Our last game we played one on one he cheated me with bad calls and cheated me by altering the score and won, and never apologized for it. I went home and stared at the ceiling. I couldn't believe he had cheated me out that game, and we never played one on one again. It took me a while to understand why he did that, and as I ventured out into life, I understood it was because *the game ain't fair*, none of it, so suck it up and play ball or get out the way and keep your head down. Basketball has shown me *the game ain't fair*, football has shown me *the game ain't fair*, school has shown me *the game ain't fair*, the workforce has shown me that *the game ain't fair*, and the streets has shown me *the game ain't fair.* If *the game ain't fair,* and especially not fair for black people, then why are we playing it? Either way, we are all born in it and have our ways of surviving it. As John H. Johnson says in his book *Succeeding Against the Odds*, he would have never got where he was by accepting no for a final answer. You will never get anywhere counting and adding up your losses. You are going to fail, and it will be your will to pick your head up and continue to search and find other ways to achieve that will keep you on the path you should be on. You are going to find yourself in some uncomfortable situations, and those will be the situations you will need to be in. Being comfortable keeps you comfortable and keeps you idle; you will never achieve any growth as an individual being comfortable. I had to step out on fragile limbs and branches with only faith at times. Don't let anyone fit you in a box; they are in that same box and cannot see themselves ever leaving that box. The box is for them and not you. Don't let yourself stop you from accomplishing what you want to accomplish; you can stop yourself sometimes. Discipline is one of the major most important lessons of life that I've learned. It is also one of the hardest traits to master because you must deny your flesh, and flesh is vulnerable and weak. I have learned to deny my flesh for months at a time and sometimes years if necessary. Like my father used to tell me as a boy, "You either want it or you don't," so stop playing with yourself if you don't really want it. And if you think someone is going to give it to you or you think someone is giving something to you, then you are lying to yourself or someone is feeding you a lie (because it will come to you in bits and pieces with limits and requirements and no real growth).

CHAPTER 11

The American Dream Is Really a Nightmare/The System I Live in

The system I live in is one where parents send their children to school in the morning and go to work shortly after, children come home from school and parents are shortly behind them or shortly before them. If you don't go to college after school, then you go to the manufacturing plants (or some other sort of "nine to five") and repeat the process that your parents did. So are teachers glorified babysitters if the average person (coming from where I come from, gifted or not) is going to just go to the factories like their parents worked in and work until you literally can't work anymore, barely keeping your head above water. And even if you go to college, then you get out with huge amounts of debt and no guaranteed job anywhere, and if you come from where I come from, you either continue living like a college student after college or you come back home and end up living like you would have if you had never ended up going to college in the first place. And if you go to the army to fight wars that you have had completely nothing to do with, then that guarantees you nothing because I have seen black men serve in the army and come home to be drug addicts. This society has said that we are fighting for the freedoms we hold dear but is never clear on what or who has those freedoms in jeopardy. Are they in jeopardy because other nations live and conduct themselves in a different manner than we do? I feel like Osama bin Laden in my own country! Black people are not yet truly free in our own country. We blacks are abundant in the lines to sign up and go to the Army, Navy, etc., because we are the ones who need the funds and jobs offered through the programs. And yet we are not really sure what we have to do with the wars. How can you be sure when police officers shoot and kill black people in the streets of America with no just cause? How can you be sure when we live in a nation that denies our potential generation after generation? How can you be sure when we are the majority in the prisons yet a minority in this country? I have made a strong case involving factual issues and factual events that the society we live needs to take a good look in the mirror and evaluate how we really live and conduct our own selves. And if the search for better is really a search for better, then why do I see so much "better" around me that is not being utilized? I see wise black men becoming drunks in the streets. I see gifted black businessmen and businesswomen not being able to go into business for themselves. I see black people with mountains of higher learning that are still only worth a minimum wage job in this society. I see black men and black women becoming drug addicts that should have been educators, great mothers, and great fathers.

You chose to take your chances and go against the odds, then you end up dead or in prison is the probability and statistic in this society. Prison is supposed to be an institution for rehabilitation, and I have seen many do prison time and hardly come back rehabilitated from anything and, in many cases, worse off than when they went in. Prisons are more like mass incarceration for black people who won't get in line and stay in their place. The statistics year after year show us blacks being the majority in the prison system, yet we are a minority in America, and the majority of prosecutors in America are white (at 95 percent). We are being incarcerated at a high rate, and families are tied to the ones being incarcerated, and the families have to endure the loss of that family member, children go without mothers and fathers, wives go without their husbands (which can present a number of problems within itself), mothers and fathers go without their children, and husbands go without their wives. So is it safe to say that the system was designed for our destruction, or is it that the system is failing black people? Pick one. So is it safe to say that we are being recycled and not utilized in this society? If we are not valued in this society, we will inevitably not see value in each other and never formulate as a people. Work for someone else until you are sixty-odd years old and enjoy the few short years you have got left on this earth as a now elderly person, and we will have your children's children do the same thing. Police officers and drug dealers working together, the drug dealer being the informant and actually the one doing the policing in neighborhoods and the inner city and the police getting credit for drug busts—so is it safe to say that the actual police officers aren't actually doing their jobs and not actually working for our tax dollars? Is it safe to say that the police's job is really just to keep black people in the place that society has put us in? Our lack of knowledge and jealousy and envy toward each other provides a smooth platform for that system. I have seen scenes being staged around me to look like actual street events and come to find out it was staged by the informant and police officer. I have seen scenes staged before in the streets to look like something that they were the total opposite of what they were. I have even had things like this happen at my job.

One day while at work, since coming back from Columbus, a supposedly known drug dealer came to my job and started an argument with me (for no apparent reason) and acted as if he wanted to fight me at my job. I ended calling some friends of mine to come down to the store just in case it got out of hand. And went out to my car and came back in with my pistol on me (I don't play around about my life especially now that I have a daughter that depends on me). He ended up leaving out the store escorted by a family member of his (right when things began to really escalate). He had another one of his partners come up to the store and start another altercation, but by this time, those friends I had called were already on the scene, and we were with whatever they wanted to do. I never called the police that day; I thought it was for something that happened in the street, so I was gonna handle it in a real street way. I ended up waiting two hours in the parking lot for them to come back after one of them left saying, "Oh, we got problems, I will be right back on G." And we waited about another hour after my store closed that night, and nobody came back, so I told my friends that I was sorry for wasting their time and went home. But when I went back and looked at the store's DVR the next day, I saw that an undercover officer was in the store during the whole thing and never revealed himself as an officer of the law. They were playing dirty, I feel, to get me fired, to turn me back to the streets, and they were simply mad because I had beaten the game and was running off with my winnings. I tell you, there is no winning in this game for us blacks. But if you were actually doing your job, then you wouldn't have to go to that extent. If you were actually doing your job instead of trying to make me lose mine, then you would have made a bust by now. Instead, I have written two short autobiographies of my life (the first is called *Risk It All: Based on a True Story*, which can be found at www.riskitallblog.wordpress.com, and the other is called *Still Succeeding Against the Odds: The Uncut Version*, which can be found at www.stillsucceedingagainsttheodds.wordpress.com), stating illegal activity that I have done, which I have posted online on blog sites. Both were posted after major runs I went on. I don't despise the system; I wish it would hold true to its word, and I wish that it worked for everyone and didn't serve the purpose of limiting and maintaining black people.

Just as the best players don't always play, the justice system is not always just. Justice isn't always served; we have seen a consistent pattern of this until the current year we live in involving black lives. And being black can be the exact thing that cuts short your greatness, and to say that we haven't had a troubled history in this country is to deny the factual points I am making. And also to say that I am the racist because I am bringing about valid issues, facts about the society we live in, is to continue to deny the issues, the facts about black lives in this society. I must say something for I have a daughter that will have to grow up in this society and I see black women growing up like whores because they see no value in themselves and black men treating black women like whores (sexually giving themselves to anyone with low standards) because they see no value in themselves and a society that supports it all because they continue to deny us our greatness. But not my daughter and not on my watch. I will continue to express matters and demand justice in all areas that we exist in.

We don't have time for their fake, purposeless, and senseless games. They are still not coming from up under the wealth that was not their wealth in the beginning. They will continue to deny us our true greatness. The purposeless games in the "real world" are just to keep us occupied and in a frozen state as they continue to make money, continue to promote the games, and maintain their well-being and wealth.

CHAPTER 12

Create Your Own System

The dominant black male will not fit in this system we live in here in America. In order to be a dominant black male in this system and create a household where you can truly be a man in and create true happiness and create true growth for you and your family, then you must create your own system. You have to create your own system in a system that is out of tune with what and who you really are. You can either stand as a man or get in where you fit in, and you know exactly where that will be for the majority of black men in this system. How do you create your own system in an already structured system? You find loopholes in the already existing system, and you capitalize on those loopholes by making the ones in authority hold true to their own laws. I would find a loophole and be in front of somebody who is eager to give me a no, and I would point out my loophole and say, "But it says right here according to your handbook that..." You make them hold true to their law, and if you have to be the one enforcing it, then do so. If you have to threaten their livelihood (their job), then do so if you have a just cause to do so. In order to create your own system, then you have to know theirs. Sometimes you have to create your own on the fly (impulsively). In order to create your own system in an already well-structured system, then you must be creative yourself. You cannot see loopholes in the system believing that the system is upholding in its entirety, and in the same breath, I would have not accomplished what I have accomplished by completely abiding by the system. The system was designed to have me go in the direction that it is comfortable with me being in, and I myself was destined to do great things. I find it very hard to play along and fall into a system that is not upholding its word and not structured for my advancements but, in fact, is structured against my advancement. In the book *Succeeding Against the Odds,* John H. Johnson tells of a time he was told by a friend of his that no black person will ever truly be free until all black people are truly free. That statement was a very true one. You cannot give me an angle in which the system will accept me and disguise it as a way to free myself. I will not be free, and furthermore, my potential is being limited. John H. Johnson created his own system to get his magazines to a circulation of 2.3 million copies a month, grossing 5.5 million dollars in 1964 from advertisement alone.

When you come from money and a system is structured for your growth, then moving about life with confidence comes very easily to that person. But when you are coming from the total opposite side of that, then confidence comes through pure will, especially when you choose a life and path that goes against the odds. Going against the odds, you will fail, and it will be your will to get back up and keep your head up that will keep you on the path toward genuine success and happiness. When I moved to Myrtle Beach during my senior high school year, I had to sit out the first few games of the season because the athletic director said that my previous coaches from my hometown had called them and told them that I had made an illegal transfer to their school and the matter was under investigation. He said they had also told him that they had plans to utilize in their program that year. I was thinking *Utilize me how? I'm not coming off the bench for nobody I know I'm better than.* I wanted to be in a program that helped me develop my skills as a player and not a program that was gonna bury my talents and say that they utilized them efficiently. So I and my father had to create a loophole by renting a house at the beach and staying in that house for a short period. I just wanted a real opportunity, that's all. In the school system along the way, I capitalized on many loopholes. I got my two AA degrees by applying for five AA degrees that I feel like I had qualified for. SJDC had accepted my transferred credits from SCSU, and I had an overlapping amount of degrees that I felt I qualified for, but no one was going to just tell me I qualified for any degrees. I applied for five and ended up getting two of them. These were actually degrees I had qualified for first coming into SJDC, and for two years there, I was unaware that I had qualified for them. As I mentioned before, I had to override the system at CWU to get my deserved playing time. If I would have relied on the system there to give me my just playing time, then I would have unjustly sat the bench on my senior year as well and thus have never become a nationally ranked collegiate player. If the system is structured for some other purpose, then call it what it is; otherwise, you are lying to society. But while I exist, I will continue to call a spade a spade and an ace an ace. I don't talk in code. If I would have relied on my job at the time I had gotten the call from the Columbus Lions, I would have never made it there. I had to go outside the law to even make that situation possible, and if I hadn't, then I would have never achieved becoming a professional athlete. And if I would have just stayed in my hometown as the system had structured for me to do, then I would have not made any of the accomplishments mentioned before possible. I went to another coast and still shined as an athlete and did it in a different sport that I had no experience in. Black people are not expected to be able to financially make such moves in life or be able to choreograph them, but the system is able to be penetrated and not because it isn't a good system. It is more because it is not an upholding system. That's besides the fact a system that can't be upholded to all its citizens' needs to always be rewritten. I made leaps and bounds in a system that would otherwise deny me, and a lot of that reason was just because I knew it wasn't a just system, and I was eager to show them that they were not the invincible Goliath that they really thought they were. I can still feel the pressure from them coming down on me for such things, but pressure is what makes diamonds, my friend.

CHAPTER 13

Putting in Work Is No Easy Task and Not for Everybody

I wouldn't advise your average person to take the path I chose to take in life. You have to be built a certain way to endure some of the things that I have. My journey started with putting in work. I was a young boy when I first starting putting in work on the basketball court. Like I mentioned before, my father would take my brother and I to the court and teach us things he had learned. But after a while my brother stopped going, it seemed that sports wasn't going to be his cup of tea. But I keep going, and my father saw in me what he saw in himself as a young man, another gifted ball player. He started to whip me into shape taking me to the track and field to run laps and get my wind up. He was taking me to the court every other day and on the weekend when he could. But it came a time where I had to start practicing on my own. My father had a family he was responsible for, and most of his time went toward those efforts. But we still had the court he had made in the backyard, and he made sure we keep a basketball goal on it. Every day after school, I was back there putting in work. Every day from elementary school to junior high school to high school, I was back there laying the foundation. After school, I was back there and at 5:00 or 6:00 a.m. on the weekend, I was back there. Out there early lacing up my sneakers and working on my left-hand layup and ball handling, working on my free throw and jump shot, working on my bank shot. I would walk up and down the street, dribbling the ball between my legs, and see how far I could go without losing the handle. I would play anybody who dared set foot back there, and most of them left with a loss. When it comes to one-on-one basketball games, I'm probably about ten thousand wins to ten losses. After all that, I would come back in the house and watch old Michael Jordan tapes. Studying what made him successful on the court and developing my mental part of the game in the process. After watching the tape, it only made me want to go back outside and try to be "like Mike." And I was lifting weights in my barn to cap the day off. So you know what I was doing all day on Saturday.

After I was denied my opportunity to play varsity for my hometown high school, I went to Myrtle Beach High School to start as a varsity basketball player, but not before those same guys that were chosen to start (in my positions instead of me) in my hometown team ended up venturing into my backyard one day. And by that time, I had put together my own varsity starting lineup. My friends and I played those guys in a three-on-three game that day and gave them a beating they should never forget. When you stepped in my backyard on my court, then you had to be ready to face the truth. I ending up moving to Myrtle Beach (knowing that I was really the truth) and had to prove myself down there as well. They had ballers down there too that felt like they should have been in the spotlight, and I wasn't just going to come down there and get handed a starting a position. So I started putting in work down there, going to outdoor courts and open gym runs to let everybody know I was the truth. In the process, I was still working on my game and lifting weights on my own time. There will never come a time where you will have to stop making your point; there will always be someone waiting to take your spot or waiting for you to slip up and make a mistake. And as I mentioned before, *the game ain't fair*, so expect anything in any arena of life. I played other players one on one. I guarded the best players. I had to let it be known that there was no doubt I was the truth. Every day in the gym at basketball practice, I played above the rim. During figure eight drills, I would finish with a dunk; during layup drills, I would finish with a dunk, and during every fast break, I would finish with a dunk. As the season played out that year, I took advantage of every opportunity and made the most of every game. We ended up losing in the third round of the playoffs; that game made me really mad because it seemed like our already known star player just gave up in the game. Why not? He already had the notoriety that he needed.

I went to SCSU and became a preferred walk-on after talking with the coach and doing some individual workouts for him. I started to come to practice every day, and again, I had to prove myself. I was dunking in every layup drill and, most times, jumping from outside the free throw line. I was going to the outdoor courts to play any competition the streets had in the area, and I would go to the outdoor courts with my cousin to work on my own game. We would have weight lifting workouts at SCSU, and I was stronger than all the other guards by far and most of the power forwards and centers too. This came from all those years of putting in that work. We had another walk-on on the team, and he and I were competing for a spot on the roster, so every day in practice while guarding each other, I had to show the coaches that I was better than him. Coach Ben Betts was the head coach at the time, and he ended up leaving to go to another university and coach that year, and I too chose to leave. I went to CJC and again had to prove myself as a player. I found myself again around a new staff and new players. I had to put in work at the opening tryouts to make myself stand out and make the team. I ended up making the team and worked all season in practice to prove myself as a player. I would often go to the gym on weekends there and work on my game and get some of the other players to come there with me to work out with me. That season, I didn't end up getting the playing time I needed to get and ended moving out to Las Vegas. In Las Vegas, I would go to Sunset Park and other outdoor courts, seeing what Vegas had to offer. I often played at the YMCA and twenty-four-hour fitness gyms throughout Vegas; I was still one of the most elite basketball players that I had run into. I started practicing with the UNLV basketball team during their summer gym sessions, and UNLV had a top-of-the-class basketball program, selecting the best players from that area and around the world, yet my talents still shined amongst them.

I started playing football at SJDC, and putting in work meant something totally different for me, the work I would be putting in would not quite be the same work and would have to be learned and developed. I had never played football until I went to SJDC, but I knew I was an athlete. I was, at times, ashamed that I didn't understand parts of the game. I didn't understand the positions, I had never watched an entire football game on any level of play, and I didn't understand the purpose or the ideology behind the game at first. My cousin who was with me only saw this as his time to finally shine over me and never took the time to try and explain to me what he already knew about the game. I was on my own, but I redshirted my first year there to learn the game and learn where I could fit into the game. I was about 215 lbs. when I first stepped on the field at 6'3", and I was advised to play linebacker. So I took my first year off and started putting on muscle; I was in the weight room most days twice a day. It was never going to be my work ethics that caused me to fail in a situation. I started watching games and studying my position. I learned the game and the purposes and goals of each position on the field. I came back that next season more knowledgeable about the game, around 240 lbs., and had got my bench press up to almost 400 lbs. My athleticism never went anywhere. I was explosive on the basketball court and explosive on the football field. I wasn't your typical football player; I can't express that enough. I had a dynamic edge and was light years better than anyone at the position. I was worked into the starting lineup my first year on the field and put up great numbers. I had no doubt that I would be getting an athletic scholarship offer. But I never stopped putting in work. After the season, I continued to work on my football skills and even joined a local Crossfit gym to keep evolving in my strength and athleticism. I worked out there for months before finally packing up and taking my talents to CWU.

Once again, I was around new players and a new coaching staff. I had to prove myself once again. I got to the university and linked up with a few other players and immediately begin utilizing the workout facilities there. This was the closest I had ever been to my dreams, and once again, it wasn't going to be my work ethic that stopped me from reaching my goal. I begin to do pool workouts to unleash new levels of speed and strength. I stayed in the weight room, and I worked out even when we didn't have practice. People would try and think of anything they could to find some flaw in my abilities, and the rumor started to float around that I couldn't squat. Squatting with a straight flat bar is a weightlifting exercise used to gain strength in your lower body to promote explosiveness in the game of football. Well, I was already explosive, but I have never been the one to disappoint. The whole summer between my senior and junior collegiate year at CWU, I worked on squatting, and at the end of the summer, I could squat 315 lbs. ten times in a set with perfect form and going all way down and up in the process. And I managed to keep my upper body strength up that summer as well. I finished my senior collegiate season as a scholarship athlete for CWU, ranking fifteenth in the nation for forced fumbles, according to NCAA.com, and had performed at a high level in different states and countries as a starter in the defensive lineup. Not too bad for a guy just outside two years from them who didn't even understand the game of football. I went on to train at Phillipi Sports Institute of Las Vegas with world-class trainers and athletes (I didn't see a better athlete there either). I trained with devotion and dedication for three months there and was completely focused the entire time. I attended a pro day at my school and attended the NFL Regional Combine at the Seattle Seahawks Facility, in both of which I displayed greatness.

I went on to work out for the Columbus Lions of the Professional Indoor Football League and once again had to prove myself and prepare myself. I went back in the lab putting in work for the event and only had a month to do so (utilizing that same weight bench I had in the barn as a child); at the time I was working in a manufacturing plant back in my hometown. I did the workout and was officially invited to minicamp by Coach Banner, director of player personnel for the organization. And I ended my career as a professional athlete there in Columbus, Georgia. I know what you think to be true, but I have never in the entire world (that I have wondered and I was consistently on the hunt) seen an overall better athlete than myself, and as honest as I have been thus far in this autobiography, that statement is as well.

I was no stranger to the workforce along the way in life as well. I have worked R&W Fashion (one of my father's clothing stores) as a sales associate in Laurinburg, North Carolina. I have worked at Pizza Hut as a delivery driver and Marley Engineered Products as a forklift operator in my hometown. I worked at Perdue in Dillon, South Carolina. I worked at the Family Dollar in Morven, North Carolina as a manager. I worked at Friendly's Restaurant in Myrtle Beach, South Carolina, in the ice cream parlor. I worked at the Dollar General in Orangeburg, South Carolina, as a stocker. I have worked at Armani Exchange as a sales representative, neighborhood Wal-Mart as an overnight stocker, and three different telemarketing companies in Las Vegas, Nevada. I worked as a security guard at nightclub venues in South Carolina and Stockton, California, as well. I worked at RadioShack in Stockton, California. I have worked as a security guard at venues in Washington as well. I have always been a businessman/entrepreneur, a hustler. I never stop putting in work no matter the platform or arena and never will stop until they shut the casket on me because hustling against the odds requires that you take no days off.

CHAPTER 14

Trying This and Trying That

When you're on the hunt for success, then you should be about willing to venture into any arena of life, especially when the majority of people around you growing up only work nine to fives. You leave this town where I am from and people expect you to come back. I have pursued an education. I have pursued a basketball career. I have pursued a football career. I have pursued several different workforce opportunities. I have pursued online businesses. I have sold several different types of narcotics, and I have hustled any product I could get my hands on and turned it for a profit. I tried this and I have tried that. This is the case for many black people in pursuit of true happiness. Turning here and turning there, risking this and risking that—that is the story of my life. I have played in many arenas of life, and most of my ventures have just turned me back to a basic life involving no real growth. This is what is commonly referred to as the trap. The trap refers to black lives being systemically structured to not exceed a certain level of growth thus having your children repeat the process that you did, and that cycle never ends. You are thus trapped in a system that will not allow you to advance in it. I have seen those who have accepted the process for what it is and never trying to go outside those boundaries. I have failed many times trying this and trying that, but one thing I refuse to do is not try. We must not stop trying. I refuse for my daughter to have to endure certain circumstances that I have when those circumstances were ultimately unnecessary. I see a lot of people that is stuck in their current state and, at the same time, have the nerve to advocate not trying to succeed in this society. Dr. Martin Luther King Jr. and other pioneers didn't sacrifice their lives for us to get to a point where we stopped trying. The foundations of the dream were set in place to see the dream manifest. We have not achieved the dream when we still experience injustices in this society. You must keep trying this and keep trying that and never stop applying pressure to the system and this society. I am now thirty years of age and have attempted more thises and thats than people in their fifties and sixties. Idleness is not an option. Do what you have to generate income for your family, but never settle. The objective is to be able to try this and try that without unnecessary barriers and unnecessary obstacles, and if you're great at what you are doing, it should be realized. The objective is to be able to be a seller, an owner, truly utilized at what are great at and not just a buyer, a modern-day slave barely surviving. In different skin, I would have been an object that society celebrated (for efforts alone) and not spit out and rejected for making achievements. If you are not trying this and trying that, then you are not trying.

CHAPTER 15

Dribble the Rock, Sell the Rock, or Rap about the Unmovable Rock

Coming from where I come from, which is the skin that a black man wears, if you want to really make it and succeed against the odds, then most likely you have to fit into one of three categories. Any other avenue is shielded off by glass ceilings or is just another flattering form of slavery (modern-day slavery). Being black in America, in many cases, is how we look at life. You can "dribble the rock," which means you can play sports and take your chances in that area because black people are notably known for their athletic ability. Making it as a successful professional athlete can possibly pay off in the millions and give you the financial freedom that we so rarely see around us. That is a vicious world that I have attested to, and obstacles await you there. Most of everyone you run into that will provide you with your next opportunity are not people who look like you. In this arena, I have witnessed Uncle Toms in full effect, trying to get what they needed from the situation, playing on being an Uncle Tom more than proving themselves as athletes, and I have seen Uncle Toms that got to play for just that reason. I always keep my dignity intact and was never willing to play that role. If I wasn't going to get the spot by my pure athletic ability, then it wasn't going to happen that way. Some coaches I ran into have even showed their disapproval at my unwillingness to be an Uncle Tom. We shouldn't have to be Uncle Toms to advance ourselves in life. In a game of competition, the better player plays (giving that he has followed the rules and is an eligible player), and if you have to be an Uncle Tom to play, then it should be called a game of Uncle Toms and not a game of competition. Call a spade a spade, and stop lying to a society and its citizens. And if the whole team happens to be black because all the better players happened to be black in every position, then let it be, and if the whole team happens to be white because all the better players are white in those positions, then let it be (we know from the history of sports in this country that all the players have been white regardless of them being better or not); after all, it is a game of competition. *Compete* is the root word in *competition*, meaning "to contend with others; to engage in a contest or competition." We were given Jackie Robinson, Michael Jordan, and Ray Lewis, only to see other Jackie Robinsons, Michael Jordans, and Ray Lewises fail, and some so badly that they returned to society after trying, never recovering from the trauma of not succeeding, only to turn to alcohol and drugs to relieve the pain, becoming addicted or worse. I have played in this arena of life myself (the world of competitive sports). I have seen "champions" put before me in several situations, and I have seen their paths end where mine could have continued to grow. I know most of them would like to feel like they are the elite of the elite and no other person could fill their shoes, but trust me, you can come to the hood and get dunked on too.

The other way that is looked at as a method of achieving true success against the odds is "selling the rock." "Selling the rock" means to sell illegal narcotics in general, selling any drugs on the street that are in demand and that you can supply to those customers. This is a method used to generate income at a higher and quicker rate than a regular job would otherwise do. If you want no limitations on your growth, then you must go outside the law to do so. And if you want to go into business legally for yourself, then selling the rock is often a method used to generate the startup for that business. John H. Johnson was in business for twenty years before he got a bank loan. He was already established for twenty years before he first got one, so if you have just got an idea and hope, then you can skip the bank as an option because America doesn't make those kinds of investments in those type of people. And good luck working a regular job trying to save the money to get your startup capital because between supporting yourself, children if you have any, and a household where you have got a car note, rent bill, light bill, and water bill, you will have just about enough gas money to get you and your car back to work that week, and the process will repeat itself week after week after week. That's why it is important to own things that can be passed down to the next generation—because the fewer bills they have, the more room they have to grow in a legit way. If you have a family house that you have the deeds to, then utilize that because if it can provide shelter for you or the next generation, then that is a place where you don't have to pay monthly rent. The same thing goes for a car; if you own a car and don't have to pay a car note, then you can save that money. Take your disposable income and build a business with it. Dribbling the rock and selling the rock are both risky businesses, but selling the rock can result in your immediate death and/or prison time. You need skills on the basketball court and football field, and you need skills to sell the rock, or you can sell the rock with the assistance of the police, which defeats the purpose of selling the rock anyway.

The last way mentioned is to rap about the unmovable rock, which means that you can rap in general as a platform to succeed against the odds. This is another form of art that black people are notoriously known for. *Rap* can be defined in a number of ways, but its general meaning is "an expression of words in the form of poetry in music-like states." In black society, rappers are often idealized for their success and their ability to create unlimited independent platforms for growth. Rap/hip-hop has influenced the world and can be lucrative. This is seen as another way to succeed in life as a black person, but it is hard to get in the rap game as well. If you don't get the attention of big record companies, then you are independent if you consider yourself a rapper. In order to support yourself independently, then you must have the capital to do so. Selling the rock is often used to support a rap career; you sell the rock to invest in a legit business. Sometimes you can dribble the rock, sell the rock, and rap about the unmovable rock simultaneously and still not succeed against the odds. And to take that fact a step further, I have two uncles on my father's side of the family that live a legit life, one of which drives eighteen-wheeler trucks for a living, the other has an extensive background in higher learning and education, and my father is the hustling guru, and between the three of them, they have not broken any generational barriers financially.

CHAPTER 16

The Art of Hustle

The definition of *hustle* is "to urge or move hurriedly along; to work busily and quickly; (slang) to make energetic efforts to solicit business or make money." If hustling were a degree, I would have been Dr. Jarrel Lee Johnson right now. There are different things you can hustle and different ways you can hustle; hustling doesn't necessarily apply to selling drugs. When you make energetic efforts to save a basketball from going out of bounds on the basketball court, then you are hustling on the basketball court. When you are making energetic efforts to advance yourself to higher playing levels of basketball, then you are hustling to pursue a basketball career. As a mentioned before, when you are skilled at hustling, then you can go in and out of hustles, maintaining them all at a high rate. The first rule of thumb in hustling anything is you got to have some "get off your behind and go." Hustling is not for the lazy and unmotivated. If you don't have the motivation to wake up with energetic efforts and end your day at night with energetic efforts, then you are not built for the life of hustling. If you don't have goals in whatever you are hustling, then you are hustling without purpose. I have made many thousands of dollars hustling different things, staying true to the basics of hustling. I have made leaps and bounds in the basketball world, football world, and the education world because I stayed true to the basics of hustling. It took hustle to make achievements in the football world, and it took hustle to be able to sell drugs in the street and see growth from them both. Just because you sell drugs, it doesn't guarantee you that you destined to come up. You have got to be good with the business end of hustling. You've got to be able to save, sacrifice, and continuously produce gains.

There is a phrase used for people who hustle and can't come up; it's called *backwards hustling*. Backwards hustlers are hustlers that cannot produce gains and see growth from their hustle. Backwards hustlers are precisely what is wrong with the hustle game today. If you are a backwards hustler, you are in the way. If you can't hustle but pretend to be one, then you need to get out of the way and let real hustlers really make some real difference out here. If you are hustling for the notoriety, then you need to get out of the way. If you are hustling to be popular with a woman, then you need to get out of the way. Black people need more genuine hustlers. We need people hustling to make a difference in the education world. We need people hustling to make a difference in the basketball world. We need people hustling to make a difference in the football world. We need people hustling to make a difference in the sports world in general. We need people hustling to make a difference in the justice system. We need people hustling to start their own business. We need more hustlers in general.

This is not the time to be idle, which is what I see on a day-to-day basis around me. The only thing they are hustling to do is to fit ones like me in the box with them. If you can devote all that energetic effort into trying to destroy me and put me in the box with you, then surely you can apply some of that effort in another area in life. I recommend you apply it to changing your own current circumstances. There is a lot of energetic effort being exhausted on a day-to-day basis around me, and it falls in either one of the two categories. You are either a hater or a hustler. Don't ever get the two confused. If you are on the block, in neighborhoods in the inner city all day, and just out there to be in the way of money being made, then you're a hater and not a hustler. If you focus on someone else's moves all day and not focus on your own moves, then you're a hater and not a hustler. If you sit around all day and watch someone leave their house and are still sitting there to watch them when they come home, then you're a hater and not a hustler. If you start selling what someone else is selling just to stop them from making that money, then you are a hater and not a hustler. If you start selling something that someone else is selling and you do it just to undercut their price and therefore cut off their income but you never stay in business, then you are a hater and not a hustler. If you come to someone's job every day just to do things to try and get them fired, then you are a hater and not a hustler. If you claim to be making more money than someone, yet you have the time to go to their job every day just to show your face, then you are a hater and not a hustler. If you set up scenes to make it seem like you are hustling just so it can look like you are making money, then you are a hater and not a hustler. If you sit around and gossip about others all day, then you are a hater and not a hustler. If you focus on someone else's relationship more than you are concerned about the person you have in your life, then you are a hater and not a hustler. If you stand by the road every day to watch somebody go to work, then you are a hater and not a hustler. If you watch what someone wears and then go and copy the outfit just to show them that you can dress well also, then you are a hater and not a hustler. If you watch someone go to the ATM every payday just to watch them get money out of it, then you are a hater and not a hustler. If you sit around and wait for someone else's downfall all day, then you are a hater and not a hustler. If you hate on someone's children because you envy them, then you are a hater and not a hustler. If you go to someone's job just to watch them clock in and smack your lips in disapproval, then you are a hater and not a hustler. In fact, you are stricken with Willie Lynch Syndrome and "crab in the bucket" mentality.

A hustler, in most cases, is just a good, solid businessman. The best hustlers can get the simplest things to hustle and, with some discipline, see gains from that hustle by just sticking to the basics and running laps with that hustle. My father was a real hustler. I never saw anyone hustle up ten thousand dollars and put it on the kitchen counter for next week's grind until I did it myself. He told me when I first got back home in 2013 (seeing that I didn't come back with much), "Son, you can't keep a hustler down." And no matter how many times I have hit the bottom, that statement has proven itself to be true. No matter how many haters lined up at the door, I still managed to make moves and see gains from those moves.

CHAPTER 17

My God-Given Right and First Amendment Right

I write this autobiography of my life (totally free of hatred for anyone and totally free of racism) because my life is a unique but necessary one. Hundreds of years before I came into existence, our country has dealt with slavery, segregation, racism, murder, stealing, and all other sorts of injustice toward black people. Every time black people stand up for themselves and decide to promote loving themselves, then suddenly we hate everybody else. Sometimes I feel like we are not allowed to love ourselves. We have to love everything and everybody else first, and then if we have got a little love left over, then we can love ourselves. It is safe to say that I am not exaggerating my life experience as a black man in America. Many of our country's noticeable marks in history have had to do with barriers being broken dealing with slavery, segregation, and racism. The world knows Dr. Martin Luther King Jr. because of his life's work dedicated to the unjust treatment of black people in America. Black people's lives are still being taken in the streets by police officers, and it is the year 2016. The only thing that is wrong with black people is what this society has done to black people, what this society continues to do to black people, what white people have done to black people, and what this system has done to black people. Our values as a people should never be in question. We have never been on the opposite side of that equation, and we should never feel like we have to prove ourselves to anyone—no system, no society—because we have not done anything as a people that deserves questioning from anybody. If anything, given the proven history with you, we should continue to question your values, your agendas, your motives—you in general. You cannot use your fear of us as a people as an excuse as to why we need to prove anything to you. I shouldn't have to "sell out" to you because that makes you comfortable with coexisting with me. Just as you are able to own and operate a business, I am also able to own and operate a business and should be able to do so (just as you are) without interference from you. We are always in situations where we have to comply with a measure that ultimately denies us our greatness as a people, and just because a few of us are sprinkled here and sprinkled there, then all of us should be happy with it despite the majority of our circumstances.

It would be completely naïve to say that in today's world, we are free of racism. Just as naïve as a person that shows me a black-owned business and tells me that there are no barriers in existence that prevent black people from owning and operating a business. Just as naïve as a person that shows me a successful black man in the corporate world and tells me that no "glass ceilings" exist in corporate America or the career work-related world. Just as naïve as a person that shows me a successful black athlete and tells me that all the great black athletes got their fair share in making it as professional athletes and/or are bearing fruit from it. Just as naïve as us seeing a few Jackie Robinsons make it in professional baseball, a few Michael Jordans make it in professional basketball, and a few Ray Lewises make it in professional football and think that when we turn on the television, we are seeing the best of the best athletes performing. Just as naïve as believing that yesterday (the past) is not connected to today (the present) and today is not connected to tomorrow (the future). Just as naïve as those who cannot make the connection between the odds that John H. Johnson faced and the odds that I faced and that those are odds put in place to keep black people from achieving real growth.

We must hustle and succeed against the odds. We must never forget our past or let it go because we have not yet achieved our natural state as a people. Everyone wants us to let go, and letting go is an invisible measure that is promoted through mass media, but letting go for us means remaining idle, never achieving being in our natural state, never seeing real growth, and never reaching our full potential and greatness in life. Why does our greatness cause fear to the rest of world? Most of our past has already been erased purposely, and if we completely let go of what past we have, we will continue to move about the world blindly, letting the blind lead the new blinds on a continuous path to destruction. We must ask ourselves why all this focus continuously remains on us. We have seen now a black president serve our nation for eight years, and yet I still see black lives being limited in growth and potential, black lives being taken by police officers of the law. As I wrote this portion of my autobiography less than a month ago, there was an incident of a black man being shot and killed by a police officer for no apparent reason in Charlotte, North Carolina, about a two-hour drive from where I currently reside. I feel the need, even the obligation, to give testaments of my own life (as I have gone against the odds) as it relates to the circumstances of the world we live in. Obligated because lies are being fed to the societies we live in—false hope, myths of opportunity, and black lives being limited in growth, potential, and opportunity.

What I do see are methods of division being placed on black lives, the potential and greatness of black lives not being fulfilled. Division disguised as truth to divide and conquer a people and make room for a lie. The risks I took are ones that were necessary ones but shouldn't have been, according to the American Dream. Mounts of achievement and still nothing. I can, I will, and I have made the argument that the American Dream is really a nightmare for us. Time after time I have proved myself when the opposition intended and expected for me to fail. True opportunity for growth is a nightmare for us. I see the methods of Willie Lynch disguised and used in different avenues and areas of life but for the same purpose. The light against the dark, the short against the tall, the young against the old, the wise against the uneducated, the rich against the poor, the famous against the infamous, the east against the west, the south against everybody, and whatever other angles that can be thought of for the division of black people. This is very evident amongst black people today; we will find the slightest differences in each other and wage war on the other. Some will spend a lifetime engaged in battle with each other. Even if those two people happen to be brothers, sisters, or brothers and sisters. The law of reproduction is that every seed produces one of its kind, the male being the one carrying the seed. Brothers can have the same father yet can still find a reason to throw one brother in the lion's den or find a reason to kill his brother. We come in different shades, shapes, and sizes just like other races, but the game of division is to continue to play on our destruction and not others. I have been able to observe this from a unique perspective, having lived in an environment like Las Vegas, Nevada, a city of three million people, where people come in many different forms, and it is a city with much infrastructure. In Las Vegas, you are not likely to encounter the same person twice in a day. And I have lived in a city like Bennettsville, South Carolina, a city of nine thousand people and a perfect contrast to a city like Las Vegas, where the interactions with each other are amplified because of the small environment. Living for years at a time in both cities, I have observed and encountered the way that black people interact with each other, and the issues we have as a people are the exact same ones in both environments.

We must educate ourselves on these matters. Once you are black, then you are black. A white person (possessing the most recessive genes of any race on the planet) and a black person (possessing the most dominant genes of any race on the planet) can produce another human being. That human being will be black in color for the dominant gene will appear. Even if the couple producing that human being happens to a white male (carrying the seed) and a black female, the child will be black, and if that child happens to be a male, then that child will be a black male who will then carry on the seed of a black male. The truth is, black people have learned to love to hate one another for someone else's agenda. The only thing we love about each other is seeing another like us trapped in the situations we can't get out of ourselves in life. This is a sick mind-set. As far as we have come, why would we be our own fools now? We are fighting each other for scraps when we are in position (that our pioneering ancestors and forefathers have put us in) to keep standing up for ourselves, and we can all sit at the mountaintop.

Willie Lynch was a vicious white slave owner in early America. He taught methods to control black slaves that could exist for hundreds of years. Methods of reducing black slaves from their natural state to create a dependency status were taught by him to other white slave owners. Methods of brainwashing black slaves to never go back to their natural state were taught by him to other white slave owners. He taught other white slave owners to concentrate on the black female and the future offspring of blacks (the nurturer and the future generation to come); he taught other slavers owners to train the black female to eat out of their hand. This meant he taught the black female to eat from the white man's hand. This can be seen in today's world for when she (the black female) goes to fill out an application, it is most likely not a black man who owns the company; when she needs that promotion in the corporate world, it is most likely not a black man giving it to her; and in general, when she needs to advance herself in life, she will most likely not be leaning toward a black man to do so. He taught that for the dominant black male slave and the most relentless black male slave to be broken so that you (the slave owner) will take him, tar and feather him, tie him to two horses, and beat the horses until they rip him apart and take the remaining black males and beat them to within an inch of their life and keep them alive for they would be useful for future breeding. Now in today's world, such things cannot be done blatantly. But if a black man that is a dominant male (in today's world), a black man that chooses to control his own income and growth by going into business for himself (legally or illegally), then he is going against the grain against the odds, and other methods will be used to make sure he gets back in his place. My life's story is a testament to such things, but although I have been railroaded in many cases and been expected to fall and never get up, I always did due to some persistent hustle. When I came back home after putting in all that work to get an opportunity to be a professional athlete and never got the call I wanted, I was expected to fall and fall hard. No matter whether it was back home or anywhere in America, after not getting to the level I had deserved to be on as an athlete, I was expected to go in a downward spiraling path and even become suicidal, turning to drugs and alcohol, but I continued to hustle against the odds. John H. Johnson (who is the founder of *Ebony* and *Jet* magazines and also the author of the national best seller *Succeeding Against the Odds: An Autobiography of a Great American Businessman* and who also inspired me to write this book, naming it *Hustling Against the Odds: A Tell-All about the Truth of the American Dream*) was an entrepreneur who attested to many unnecessary obstacles in his pursuit of establishing his own business and a multimillion-dollar company. Methods like this were displayed for all the other black slaves to witness so they could witness what happens when you go against the grain. I can make the same case for my life; it is a life that you can understand through this book what going against the grain gets you. You must be strong to take a path such as mine or my father's or John H. Johnson's, and most are not willing to do so, but there must be some who do, and for some who do, there are some that fail terribly and are made an example of in many ways. Those that try and fail and never get up in today's world are examples for other black people to see; to see that, you must stay in line or God forbid such things will also happen to you. For the black female he, Willie Lynch, also taught that the slave owner should test her in every way to see if she will submit to your every will; if not, then beat her within an inch of her life and she will make her offspring submit to you as well to be dependent like her. In today's world, you often see the black woman stand against her man in the home and often not support him, and she still raises her kids up to conduct themselves in that manner also. When she cannot completely have her way, she knows exactly who to call, and that is the police. When he is hustling or doing something illegal and she can't completely have her way, then she knows exactly who to call, and that is the police. He taught that with the black male image destroyed (a man denied being a man and is now in a childlike position). The black female will be frozen in her state; she will train her female offspring to be as psychologically dependent as her. In this state, she will be left out front, leaving the black male scared behind her and exactly how God didn't want a family to be structured. So if we now know this, then we also know the black man was meant to be a strong man who was in charge of his household, able to provide for them without assistance or dependency on any white person. This is an impossible task in today's society for any black man, for even if a black man is able to provide for his family, then he must do so dependently, in some form or fashion, on a white individual, which comes to be some type of obedience and submission. If we know this, then we know that it is also impossible for a black man to fully take charge of his household (which, as mentioned before, is the way that God intended it to be). If we know this, then we know that black households, with the exception of very few, are dysfunctional households, which is primarily the reason that black fathers are notoriously not in their children's lives—because they can't be men in their own homes (he is only another child, and the black woman often leads the household through misdirection and confusion) because he has been reduced to an infidel. In today's world, the black woman often generates just as much income or more than the black male; she often is more educated and has better employment than he does. We must return to our natural state as a people the black man, the black woman, and their offspring. The only purpose I have seen in my thirty years on this earth for two or more black people to come together for was to hate on another black person and then go off and secretly hate each other. I have seen fathers jealous of their own sons, mothers envious of their own daughters, brothers fight and kill one another. All this attention is still on black lives in today's world because in black people, there is a greatness like seen in no other, greatness that if let loose will shine and impact the world, leaving everything else to seem secondary in its path.

But through all of that, I see a force behind the matter and contradictions that can shine light on the truth. I see the truth being buried and people who claim to know a thing or two because they stole a thing or two. The Bible clearly describes the Son of God's appearance in the good book and the days on which the older days took place, yet I only see images of white gods in the society we live in. White gods on candles, white gods on T-shirts, white gods on church buildings, church windows, and other church items. Tell me, how can you steal a god? If you are willing to steal a God, then surely stealing a Super Bowl isn't beneath you, when all the money, power, resources, and law are in your favor, or putting the ones you want in the NFL, fair or not. And the same goes for the NBA, MLB, BET, MTV, and any other organizations or media where an image is displayed. The same can be said for the workforce and other avenues of generating income. Why put a white god in a religion(s) that clearly describes him as being something very unlike white? Why steal a Super Bowl? For the same reason we (blacks) were not allowed to play sports with whites, use the same public restrooms as whites, go to the same schools as whites, etc. All signs point to a need to feel superior, feel important. I can, I have, and I will make a strong case for surviving where surviving means saving your image, your race, because you somehow feel that a white person is a more evolved, superior human being even when, despite unnecessary choreographed barriers and obstacles, other races still accomplish what they accomplish, get degrees they get, create what you create, play the sports you play, and in many cases, are better than you. For this is the reason for my autobiographies—I stand before you with little to no help from any systems of the government or whites in general (more on the side of none, but there have been individuals who helped and displayed genuinely good acts of humanity), but I am a high school graduate, a college graduate with two AA degrees, a university scholarship athlete, a NFL Regional Combine interview selectee, and in NCAA ranked fifteenth in the nation and made it to the level of a professional athlete. I have worked fifteen-plus jobs in my life, and yet I still live below the poverty line in America (and without a relentless will would have absolutely nothing) because (and I have made several cases) I refuse to get in a line that I don't deserve to be in and a line that someone that shouldn't have been in charge of that line in the first place has put me in. Getting in line would have denied me my greatness accomplished thus far; getting in line would only have continued to enable an already disastrous world full of never-ending war and injustices.

When you have the most recessive genes of any other race, then you must segregate yourself, whether through visible measures or invisible measures, in order to preserve your image. In today's world where the World Wide Web exists and cameras on phones exist, invisible measures are necessary to "keep your face clean" when you want to preserve your image. You cannot tar and feather a black man and tie him to two horses and beat the horses until they rip him apart; it would not rub over well with the world. I am all for everyone existing in the way that they are. The only thing wrong with that is preservation for you comes at the expense of everyone else (by your choice and hand), especially with the black race possessing the most dominant genes of any race on the planet. So is it right for our greatness to be cut short and our children's potential to be cut short, and ultimately, for the destruction of the world to make room for a lie? I say very boldly, *no!* I will give you an example of such things: If an isolated town of one thousand white people (variable A) and one thousand black people (variable B) coexisted with no predisposition of race, with no barriers, no segregation, no lies existing, then over time, surely, inevitably, you will have a town of nothing but black people (variable B). This is not my fault, but these are the facts.

A society that conducts itself in such a manner as ours should not be called a society at all. For ones that are willing to steal a god, steal a Super Bowl, etc., to make room for a lie, those that are in control of towns, cities, states, nations, and the world, then what can be said about the truth of the organizations, sanctuaries, and laws that we as citizens of the world depend on to be upholded and true? And because of the forces of the world, we are destined not to survive independently of such things.

The way of life we are living as a society and a world is not a healthy one. The world itself is beginning to deny the existence of such cancers to the world. When Earth denies your ways, there will be no need to go to Mars because she never birthed you and will immediately reject you. Why destroy earth through such ways of living, build your technology, and go to Mars, when we have a utopia here on Earth if we conduct ourselves in a healthy manner? Am I supposed to sit back, let you (disguised as a savior) sell me a sandwich with cancer in it, take the resources of the earth from the profits, and go to Mars with it? Or maybe that's exactly what I should do. The ways of the world will work itself out in its own manner and don't need your assistance to do so; the designer of it made it that way. We are on a one-way path to destruction; the world is doing things and reacting in ways that it has not done in many years. Glaciers are melting that have been glaciers for many years. The earth's atmosphere is starting to deteriorate and, therefore, expose us more to the sun. It is our way of life that is responsible for this; unhealthy man-produced toxins are being pumped into the atmosphere, causing it to deteriorate. You are in search of answers that you will never have the answers to and are trying to figure out something that God already has the answers for. You need to sit down, and someone needs to sit you down (but I'm sure God has his time for that). Just because you can stitch a human being doesn't mean that you can act as if you can make one yourself from scratch, and it doesn't mean that you are a lifesaver, and it doesn't give you the right to play God. God's law is God's law and not man's to tamper with. Do yourself a favor and sit down and save yourself in the process. We must not be man pleasers, for if I had been a man pleaser, I would not have accomplished what I have accomplished thus far in life. Artificial foods and preservatives have caused cancers in food and, thus, cancers in us. Sit down and let the food grow the way God intended it to grow. I don't want it quicker or bigger; I want it as it was meant to be. And I'm going to speak on my daughter's behalf and say that she doesn't want it that way either. Cancer and diseases that are new to the world exist today because new things are being done in the world. We are starting to exceed the boundaries of what man was meant to do, and as those ways continue to grow, the world will continue to grow in denial of such ways.

CHAPTER 18

Contradictions and Truth

Contradictions must be highlighted to shine truth on these situations. People in the world are saying that the weak are the watered-down ones but these are the same people with the most recessive genes on the planet that are pushing that agenda; that's a contradiction. We know that white people have the most recessive genes of all the races and black people have the most dominant genes of all the races. If we know that black people possess the most dominant genes of any race on the planet, then we know that any other race that reproduces with the black gene will, in fact, produce a black person. I don't need a DNA test to tell me that. If we know that if black people possess the most dominant genes of any race on the planet, then we also know that black people must have been the first original human beings on the planet and that every other race is just another form of that original race, including the fact that any two human beings can reproduce with one another. I can go to the exact opposite side of the world and reproduce with another human being that is a female; if my sperms are not defective and she is capable of bearing a child, then we can very well make another human being despite our outside appearances. Since we know that, then we know that all human beings are, in fact, human beings and outside appearance is not an indication that we have evolved into something different from one another. But what we do know is that the outside appearances commonly found in black people are an indication of ones that are direct descendants of that original race. The way we look is a reflection of the environment that our ancestors have stayed in and how God made us. If we know that black was the original race of people and we know that Africa is the continent in which black people are predominantly found, then we know that black people come from Africa, and thus all human beings have our origins in Africa and Africa is the birthplace of the most ancient of things known to man, including the Great Pyramids, and everything else that has come into existence since is just another form of those ancient things. So it is no coincidence that the oldest human remains were found on the continent of Africa or that it is still unknown to present man how the Great Pyramids were constructed (so are they driving the world forward or backward toward a cliff?). If we know that the black race was the first race of human beings, then we know that all knowledge and wisdom of the world has its origin from that first original race. If we know that the black race was the original race on this planet, then we know that all great athletes have their origins from that original race of people. So it is hard to make it seem like I am not capable of comprehending what you can comprehend because you are a different shade of black (another race). And it is also hard to make it seem like I am not capable of playing the sports you play because of my outside appearance. If we know that the black race is the origin of everything on earth created by man, then we should now understand why we haven't seen a Lebron James, a Michael Jordan, a Jackie Robinson, a Ray Lewis, or a me produced from any other race on the planet to date. We should now understand why the best singers, dancers, etc., are commonly found in black people. Might I add it feels good to be in tune with the earth; otherwise, I would try to make a run for Mars and drive the earth backward off a cliff in the process.

We should also understand now why such things of our past have been done to black people by other races. We should now understand that it was no coincidence why we have been torn from our history, knowledge, wisdom, land, and tongue. But the things we have been torn from have their ways of coming back around in different forms that reflect those exact same things that we have been torn from us in an inevitable fashion. God was flawless in his design, so ultimately, they will have no say in it. We should now understand why we had to fight for civil rights in our own country. We should now understand that the "scramble for Africa" was not a coincidence, nor was slavery in America or any other account in history where black people have been targeted for destruction. We should now understand why black people were not allowed to play sports with white people in the beginning of sports history in this country. We should now understand why black people's greatness is constantly, consistently, and systemically cut off from the world. We should now understand why black people in this country, a country that promotes higher learning, have died with a wealth of knowledge that was systemically cut off from the world. We should now understand why black people were not allowed to read or write in this country—might I add it feels very good to be writing this book? We should now understand why I feel the need to systemically give the world this truth as it relates to my own life experiences.

I can't help but highlight the contradictions of the world as they relate to the real-life experiences I have had myself as a black man living in this world. So first and foremost, a man pleases a woman sexually with his penis and not his testicles, so a man with pants full of testicles and no substantial-sized penis is not "packing" anything. This is an invisible measure that has been created to evolve the world around, to maintain a reason for a certain image's existence, and sell us a sandwich in the process. Somehow, according to stigma and them, how large a man's testicles are determines how much courage and heart he possesses. I would like to see the scientific correlation for that. A man's testicles serve the purpose of carrying sperm and the seed that he uses to impregnate a woman with. If he is able to do that, then his testicles work just fine and have served the only purpose they have, and to think otherwise is a contradiction. Well, what is to be said of women with no testicles? Can they not handle any pressure put upon them adequately? We know from barriers that women have broken in this society and accomplishments they have made that this is contradiction. This "invisible measure" is used to discriminate against woman and their possible potential to contribute to a society and, furthermore, to promote racism and racial division to ultimately promote white superiority. Only the real and those not watered down can eat and survive the stigma being promoted on television ads and modern television shows, yet in the real world, I see black people who consider themselves really living paycheck to paycheck and even completely broke; that's a contradiction according to the stigma being forced on society. This is besides the fact that when we (blacks) protest in the streets under the title "Black Lives Matter," the topic of "All Lives Matter" seems to overwhelm the cause, but this is a contradiction in a society that promotes "Only the Strong Survive." If there are strong people, then there must be weak people that are not allowed to survive, so how does "All Lives Matter" work again? They make it seem like you are non-American or anti-American if you don't play along with their game, but they aren't playing even close to fair or by their own rules; that's a contradiction. That's why it's important to highlight these contradictions—because the truth of the matter is they don't want us standing up for ourselves and highlighting the fact that our greatness is being trapped off and cut short. What I do see are a people that can exist if they play along with the game. If you go outside of that, then you are destined for extinction. So dare not to go against the grain because your children's children will pay for it, if that generation makes it here.

I have had those tell me that I have not "come off the porch" yet, meaning that I have not left the nest of my comfort zone. The porch represents the portion of the house that a person dare not leave because of his fear of what is beyond the porch, just as a baby bird doesn't leave the nest until it is ready to fly. This was said even after I left this entire country and went to another country and performed as an athlete in that other country. These are the type of contradictions fabricated to continue to deny me and those like me our true greatness. This world is full of contradictions. Being black in a world of contradictions, yes doesn't mean yes and no doesn't mean no; yes means no, no means yes, right is often wrong, wrong is often right, stay means go, go means stay, black means white, white means black, up means down, down means up, right means left, left means right, lie down means get up, get up means lie down, good means evil, and evil means good.

Control is the only way a race with the most recessive genes on the planet can preserve their image and, at the same time, coexist with others. You must control everything—the religion, the sports, the super bowl, the money, the law, the order, the system, the town, the city, the state, the nation, the world, and even the outlawed streets and street gangs. And the ones who support it, don't say anything about it, and continue to benefit from it are just as guilty as the most powerful ones who institute these controlling measures. People moving outside the law's long arm are a prominent threat simply because their moves are not monitored. Your capital is not controlled and limited, and therefore, your growth cannot be controlled and limited. Most street gangs were formed in order to establish some sort of independence from the government. Most street gangs were formed to establish some sort of neighborhood protection from the police. Most street gangs nowadays have been infiltrated by the government and police of America through methods of confidential informants. They control the streets now, and most gangs have been diluted down to organizations that were formed to be independent but are now dependent of the government and police and cannot make moves independent of authorities. This agenda is promoted through mass media as well; I have yet to understand what a blue blood is. They control the streets and promote doing so through mass media so their gang, the Blue Bloods, can continue to regulate, control, and move as they do.

The same can be said for a businessman that owns and operates his own business, for if he does own a business, there must be glass ceilings put in place and limitations on his growth. And for a society that fears the growth, economically and monetarily, of a people with the most dominant genetics on the planet for reasons of their own image and race's survival, then that society must control the outlawed streets through such methods as confidential informants and control the world of business/entrepreneurs by controlling the distribution of such resources, law, and capital to do so. So it is no coincidence why the inner city is predominantly black and poor and there are so few black businessmen that own and operate in the common market. It is no coincidence that the manufacturing plants are filled with black workers, yet there are few successful black businesses; few blacks own and operate banks, grocery stores, clothing stores, and other organizations of infrastructure in black communities. In my own community, in every corner, I see stores being operated by whites, people of Middle Eastern descent, and Asian descent, and the majority of customers buying products daily are black. They buy products and going to work, make the money, and give it back. Where is the room for real growth? There is none. The majority of blacks see nothing wrong with it until they see someone who looks like them behind the counter getting the money. I myself currently, as mentioned earlier, work as a manager in a retail business establishment and have experienced full-blown Willie Lynch Syndrome alive today in a business that is not even my own, but it's just a matter of the fact that I'm getting a portion of that money.

The good book states that God says it is from a lack of knowledge that my people are destroyed, and every day in society, I see a lack of knowledge destroying black people. *Nigger* was the name given to us, meaning "an ignorant person." How does a wise, once fruitful people become niggers? These things can be read about in books that subject you to "The Scramble for Africa," "Slavery in America," the "Civil Rights Movement," etc. You detach them from their homeland, you destroy all their civilizations, you destroy their tongue (their language), you divide them, you devise methods to keep them that way, and you will forever have a true nigger, but you don't completely destroy them, for within them are educators you can steal from and learn from and call your own—doctors and healers, wise men and wise women, and athletes like no other. I know of wise black men who have died; buried with them was a wealth of knowledge. And in the same breath, I have witnessed black athletes of Lebron James's caliber that I have yet to see produced from any other race of people, but I myself make a yearly salary that's below the poverty line, so who am I to mention such things? I feel that God made us with melanin for a reason for even the dirt has melanin in it, and since the good book tells us how he created us from the dust of the ground, I know he made us with melanin for a reason; he was flawless in his design. It has been man's history of going against

God's law that has us on the path we are on to destruction, and the continuing denial of God's law in favor of man's law will be our ultimate destruction. And to continue to deny me is to continue to deny God's law.

For if there was truly an equal playing field, then there would be too many of us shining and not enough of them shining, and following would be an undeniable impression on the world. As a gifted young basketball player myself, I never made it past the collegiate level of play and understood when people would say that there were Michael Jordans in the inner city. Meaning that there were other black men who played basketball at Michael Jordan's caliber who never made it to his level of play, who still lived in such parts of America below or near the poverty line for such reasons I have mentioned before. And to take that fact a step further, I also now know that there are Ray Lewises in the inner city making it to a professional team like myself but never seeing that growth fully manifest and never bearing fruit from it for such reasons that I mentioned before. As I am a college graduate with two AA degrees, I still never received my bachelor's in business management, which I studied for at Central Washington University, although I got accepted into the school of business there, which was considered a hard thing to do, as Central Washington is known for their school of business accreditation. I never completed it for such reasons and obstacles I mentioned before (it not being a favorable thing for a black man to be associated with business or own a business in this society) as John H. Johnson also attests to in his national bestseller, *Succeeding Against the Odds*. The path was made unnecessarily difficult, and I never received my bachelor in business management, but I stand before you today in the role of a manager in a business establishment and have done so adequately thus far. And to let John H. Johnson know, there are still some who are succeeding against the odds. I can also go to the extent of saying that when I first walked into this establishment, we were ranked the eighteenth store out of nineteen stores in the district, and within six months of me being there, we moved up into the number one store in the district despite unnecessary obstacles in the "real world," and have consistently ranked amongst the top since then. Might I add that this is another contradiction: being found inadequate to get a business management degree but performing successfully in the role of a manager in a business in the "real world" for approaching a year now.

It is not just me—black people's greatness across the world is being cut short for such reasons mentioned before. And I am not one to sit back and say nothing while we (blacks) fill the factories working on assembly lines like recycled useless robots, making $15,000 to $30,000 yearly, yet we are able to contribute to society in the same and often better ways than ones who occupy $100,000 and up yearly salary occupations. Sit back and say nothing while ones disguised as champions are given to society as true champions while the inner city is filled with real champions who will never be recognized as true champions in this society. We black people are getting a cold deal around the table. I know because I am black and I have been around the table. They will keep the wealth because keeping the wealth means keeping control. Keep controlling the mass media that influences the way we think and the way our kids will think and influence their life choices to align with the system, but deny their true potential. Keep controlling the world so you can dictate what is accepted and what is not accepted. Keep control and keep us dependent. Keep control and keep us from achieving our natural state as a people. Keep control and keep the lie going. Keep control and keep your image as an image that is superior. If I say nothing and play along, then I can survive, but if I say something about it or bring notice to the matter, then I'm soft or weak and not allowed to survive. That's a contradiction. If I stand up for myself against tyrants of people with numerous resources—the law of land at their disposal, the nation's armed forces at their disposal—then that shows strength, not weakness. The strong among us blacks are the ones who dare chose to succeed against the odds, and the weak ones are those who say nothing, play along, and keep their head down. Society's agenda of saving hope is really saving themselves at anyone's expense, especially ours, and I am using my God-given right and my First Amendment right to say something about it, no matter the consequence I have already experienced and am fully aware of. If you have read my first autobiography online (*Risk It All: Based on a True Story*) and the first chapters of this book, then you will see that I am one of those children's children who dared to go against the grain. The world around me continues to make excuses for me and other blacks not truly succeeding and excuses for the glass ceilings I keep running into, but I continue to look at the facts, and I continue to see contradictions.

When my father got locked up, he had a Corvette that was his prized possession; it was burgundy in color and had many customizations done to it from the motor to the body of the car. That was one of the items they took when they made that bust on him. A few months after taking the car, the police department put the car up for auction, and my father had his brother go to the auction and buy that Corvette back. When the police caught drift that it was his brother that had bought the Corvette back, they came and repossessed the car again. But when my father got out of prison, he went into business for himself as an entrepreneur. He did it the legit way; he got his business license, and his startup money was legit money. He opened a clothing business and starting doing what he did best—he hustled. He worked hard and honestly and saved up enough money to buy him another Corvette, and this time it was a white one and it was nice. He was very proud of that Corvette because he had hustled up the money in an honest way. But lo and behold—here came the local police again, after several years of my father being a law-abiding citizen, with a warrant to search our house for the illegal selling of films. They didn't find any illegal movies, but they did find a shotgun in my father's closet. He had it for the protection of our family, but it wasn't a good enough reason when he was a convicted felon still on probation. The local authorities gave my father a decision to make: he had a choice between going back to prison to finish out his time for violating his parole or he could (of course) give them the Corvette. It was an easy decision for my father, who had already been gone for several years and didn't want to leave us again, so they drove off with the Corvette. My father told me that it hurt him most to see them take that Corvette because he hadn't done anything illegal to get that one. He didn't let that stop him; he continued to hustle, and today he has a red Corvette, and he got it before he became a minister. But he is, in fact, a minister today and his business card has "Minister Ronnie Lee Johnson" on it. I would like them to try and come up with a reason that they justify to the public to take that Corvette. As a pastor, he discourages illegal activity of any kind and gives back to the community in many ways. He has built his congregation up and has done many renovations and upgrades to the facilities of the church building. He has brought the church a new church van and built the church's treasury up to tens of thousands of dollars. But as I see things play out around me, it still seems to not be enough. They still have it out for our family and continue to try to divide us, and as I mentioned before, the game they play isn't fair. My grandmother has passed, as I mentioned before, and she had a house that was paid for. The lights are currently not turned on and have an overdue bill. My mother has been to the local electricity company, and even after she proved she was an heir, they refused to switch the bill over in her name so that we could keep the house up and let future generations live there. The last time she went up to the electricity building to talk to someone, the manager in charge saw her pulling in the parking lot and hurried back in the building and went into her office and closed the blinds and told her coworkers to tell my mother she was busy. They angle informants (friends and family) at us. Women come into my and my brother's lives just to try to demonize us as people because we are our father's sons. They stage destruction around us daily, and we are still not yet free of the rift they have sought out against us for going against the odds. My oldest brother, as I write this, is living in a house with no lights on and leans toward alcohol as a way to relieve the pain he has encountered and encounters daily. Me, personally, I keep my "they" block on, and it is hard to penetrate it. *Succeeding Against the Odds* by *John H. Johnson* was a book that my father read while in prison, and he gave that same book to me when I came back from Columbus, Georgia, seeing that I had taken another fall in life and this time I had a family involved that fell with me. He has three sons and a daughter and could have given the book to either one of us, but he saw fit to give it to me, and I am thankful for it. From one Johnson to another, I understand why John H. Johnson chose to name his book *Succeeding Against the Odds*. If he had never gone outside the lines he was persuaded to live in, then he would have never built a multimillion-dollar business and established true happiness for his family. If he had never hustled against the odds, then he would have never succeeded against the odds.

CHAPTER 19

Build Your Own Businesses and Infrastructures

There were people who said I didn't belong in the "real world" and made college seem like the path I should take, but when I chose to study business, it became an unnecessarily difficult task; that's a contradiction. As we now feel the need to record and document police brutality on blacks for true justice, I can and have made the case that is also very important to document such achievements on the basketball court, football field, the workplace, and the classroom for true justice. In the Bible, 1 Timothy 1:8 states that we will know that a law is a good law if man uses it lawfully. The world has witnessed America's injustice against blacks for many years back, up until the current year we live in, so what is that to say about the law of America and the people who control and dictate that law? A law that can't hold true to itself by its enforcers of that law should not be abided by anyone. It is important for black people to always keep their heads up and always hustle. If we were valued in this country in the way that we should be and not trapped off and consistently railroaded into glass ceilings, then we wouldn't have to build our own infrastructures, but still, until this present year, it is a necessity to pursue. Pursue your finances, own things you can hand down to the next generation, build businesses and your own infrastructures, gain resources, and don't let them divide and conquer you. When you're hustling or doing something illegal to make money, your objective should always be to come up, go legal, and build a legit business. We cannot stay dependent on a system that denies us our growth. We cannot stay dependent on infrastructures that deny us our growth. We cannot stay dependent—period. Dependency will continue to deny us our natural state as a people. We must make progress toward some independency.

You don't have to always come up the illegal way, but working a nine-to-five will take some tremendous sacrifice; the way those jobs are set up are to keep you coming back to work, living paycheck to paycheck. You will work until you are in your sixties and draw your 401k plan, and by then you can't enjoy the money like you could have in your thirties or forties. Your life would have been done and passed you by. So most times, you are going to have to do what you got to do, come up, go legal, and build a legit business to keep you going at a rate where your money and growth can't be limited. Employ some of the real, genuine loyal people you met along the way, and put them in positions with salaries that would have been denied to them in the "real world." Repeat that process, and build your own infrastructure and other institutions that you can trust and rely on in your community until you establish yourself as your own entity. Then maybe you can be respected in the way that you should be. That is easier said than done for every successful black business that has made it. Their methods of success have been broken down and studied, and new methods of rebuttals for such things have been instituted in the system; trust me, I know all my life I have been hustling against the odds. But building your own businesses and infrastructures is very well possible with some persistent hustle. As I mentioned before, I see white-owned businesses, Middle Eastern–owned businesses, and Asian-owned businesses operating with no interference. But when a black person decides to establish his own business in a country that promotes the spirit of entrepreneurship, which is exactly what the American Dream is all about, then we are soft and anti-American. It seems to me that we are only allowed to be the workers and are, in fact, the modern-day slaves.

CHAPTER 20

Dreams of a Hustler

I just want to be great for God intended me to be that way. I want to be great with no excuses as to why my greatness is denied. And no matter what excuse you come up with to deny me my greatness, I can rebut it with the truth. My greatness, if not trapped off and cut short, will set bars that will drive the world forward toward true greatness. If my greatness is not trapped off and cut short, I will rank in the top amongst the nation. I never asked for unnecessary obstacles in my life, but they were there, and no one coerced me into writing this book; this is how my life panned out before me as I pursued my greatness, and it just so happened to end up (thus far) similar to my father's. Yes, I have accomplished a lot in my life thus far, but I have not seen a lot of my potential manifest into what it could have been because of the forces of the society we live in. I want to see all greatness fulfilled, no matter what form it comes in. There will be many who oppose what I say in this book despite the facts I mentioned, and the opposition will continue to lie to society, but I have witnessed with my own eyes from within my own family and other black lives greatness and potential being cut short and a lie being groomed into its fullest form and given to society as the truth. They will continue to lie and continue to deny black people our greatness. So I will continue to protest for our greatness and to be able to say that I have lived a full life on this earth and lie on my dying bed knowing that my children will also have an undeniable opportunity to fulfill their lives and potential. I want to see the world rid of contradictions and unnecessary barriers. I don't want to live my life full of unnecessary risks; I just want to live my life. I don't want to feel like I'm on the run in my country because I'm standing up for the truth. I don't want to work for you and your wicked agendas for my whole life and then disposed of when I can't work anymore and the only purpose my children will have is to repeat that process. I don't want a war, but in the current year we live in, I still feel the need to be war-ready. I don't want to live dependent on anyone, especially those who do not have my best interest at heart. I don't want to live in a system that is structured against me; I want to live in a system that is structured for me. I wish we all could come together as one society with true justice that applies to all in the same manner. I want to live in a world where all people can trust the law and law enforcers. I want to live in a world that is free of jealousy and envy. I want to live in a cancer-free world. I don't want to live in the state that you want me in; I want to live in my natural state, how God intended me to live. I want to live in a world where our daughters are not reduced to whores but see their lives fulfilled as the queens they were meant to be. I don't want to see our sons fill your prisons and be blocked away from the world; I want to see them stand in their homes and in the world as the kings they were intended to be. I don't want to have my life destroyed because someone else is trying to figure out their place in the world. I would love to live in a world like this and wish I could be here when that world exists.

Word in Quotations Defined

Hustle: To urge or move hurriedly along; to work busily and quickly; (slang) to make energetic efforts to solicit business or make money.

Game: The playing field of life.

African American: A black person who resides in America.

Caucasian American: A white person who resides in America.

Re-up: Buying more products to sell.

Backwards Hustling: Hustling in a way that is nonproductive. Unable to produce fruit and/or gains from your hustle.

Getting my weight up: Buying more and more product to sell thus getting more weight of the product; doubling up on new purchases.

Connect or Plug: The person that supplying the product.

Crackhead: A person who is addicted to crack cocaine.

Cokehead: A person who is addicted to cocaine.

Weedhead: A person who is addicted to marijuana.

Hitting a lick: Serving product to a customer.

Dirty: To have narcotics in your possession or be around narcotics.

Work: The actual product being sold.

Play: A move being made in the streets in other to sell product.

Hood: Inner city parts of a town or city where black people reside.

Mrs. Midgleys: White people who practice racism and/or support racism and/or discriminate for reasons of skin color.

Bouncing back: Making a return to a stable position in life financially or regaining back what you once had before.

Lol: Laughing out loud.

Race: A term used to divide human beings.

Invisible measures: Stigma and/or methods of brainwashing place on society to believe in something that is not true through methods like television shows, television commercials, and other forms of mass media.

Real world: Places that exist in society that believe in and/or support invisible measures.

Go-getter: A person that relentlessly pursues their goals, finances, dreams without limitations.

Uncle Tom: A black person who kisses ass to advance themselves in life.

Real nigger: A black person that has been detached from their homeland, detached from their native civilizations, denied their tongue their language, divided from people of their kind, and brainwashed and/or is cognizant of remaining that way.

Willie Lynch Syndrome: A syndrome-type mentality instilled in black people, passed down from generation to generation, that reflects the methods practiced, condoned, and taught by Willie Lynch, who was a vicious white slave owner in early America. He taught methods to control black slaves that could exist for hundreds of years. Ways of thinking/ways of surviving like dark versus light, old versus young, and the woman versus the man (the differences) were installed in black slaves through rigorous methods. Ways of thinking like trusting only white people were instilled in black slaves (from the man to the woman to the child) through rigorous methods. Methods of reducing black slaves from their natural state to create a dependency status were taught by him to other white slave owners. Methods of brainwashing black slaves to never go back to their natural state were taught by him to other slave owners. He taught other slave owners to concentrate on the black female and the future offspring of blacks, to train the black female to eat out of their hand. He taught that for the dominant black slave male and the most relentless black male slave to be broken, you (slave owner) must take him, tar and feather him, tie him to two horses, and beat the horses until they rip him apart, and take the remaining black males and beat them to within an inch of their life and keep them alive for they will be useful for future breeding for future slaves. Methods like this were displayed for all the other black slaves to witness. For the black female, he also taught that the slave owner should test her in every way to see if she would submit to your every will; if not, then he must beat her within an inch of her life and she will make her offspring submit to you as well to be dependent like her. He taught that with the black male image destroyed, the black female will be frozen in her state; she will train her female offspring to conduct and be psychologically dependent as her. In this state, she will be left out front, leaving the black male scared behind her—exactly how God didn't want a family to be structured.

Crab in the bucket mentality: A mental state of mind that refers to multiple crabs being in a bucket and one crab climbing out of the bucket but is pulled back in by another crab.

ABOUT THE AUTHOR

Jarrel Lee Johnson is the author of the autobiography *Hustling Against the Odds: A Tell-All about the Truth of the American Dream*. He was inspired to write *Hustling Against the Odds* due to the unique life he has lived thus far. The book is about his life until now, as he ventures through the world in pursuit of an opportunity against the odds that a black man faces in America. He has lived in ten cities and five states and has had the opportunity to visit another country. He is an high school graduate, has played college basketball, has played college football, has earned an academic scholarship to go to college, has earned an university athletic scholarship, was ranked fifteenth in the nation for forced fumbles concluding his senior collegiate year at Central Washington University according to NCAA.com, has attended a pro day at the university in which he earned his athletic scholarship, has attended the 2013 NFL Regional Combine at the Seattle Seahawks Training Facility in which he was selected following his workout to do an interview with the Q13 Fox News, was recruited by the Columbus Lions of the Professional Indoor Football League to continue his career as a professional football player, and has performed as an athlete in arenas around the world. He is a college graduate with two AA degrees, one of which is in arts and humanities, and the other in elementary education teacher preparation, and he has a daughter who is one year old, going on two years of age. *Hustling Against the Odds* is a tell-all about his journey as he broke down barriers and made his mark on the world, coming from a small town.

www.ingramcontent.com/pod-product-compliance
Lightning Source LLC
LaVergne TN
LVHW091107150826
845673LV00002B/740

9781635685947